WE'VE ONLY JUST BEGUN

OREGON TRAIL DREAMIN' BOOK ONE

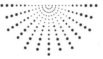

KATHLEEN BALL

CHAPTER ONE

*S*usan jounced in the saddle as the horse careened through the streets of Independence, Missouri. Being jarred sideways, she grabbed for the pommel but her sweat-slicked fingers began slipping off. Another good jolt and she would find herself beneath Sunshine's hooves. Frantically grasping the pommel with a solid hold, Susan closed her eyes and said a quick prayer. Her life couldn't end this way, it just couldn't. It had been a struggle to make her way to Independence. It was supposed to be a brand new start.

"Umphh." Strong arms wrapped around her ribs and hauled her out of harm's way. His firm grip hurt but it was much better than being run over by a horse. She found herself practically sitting on the stranger's lap while he held her tight against him. His hard chest and the warmth of his body made her forget her pain. She'd barely been able to catch her breath until he slowed his horse. She gasped when she found herself moving through the air again as he handed her to another man on the ground.

Once free of the other man, she turned to thank her savior and was dumbstruck. She opened her mouth to thank him but words escaped her. She'd never seen a man so tall before. He towered over her by a few feet. Slowly she worked her gaze up from his dusty boots, along his legs that seemed to go on forever, to his trim waist and then to shoulders as broad as a barn. She gulped. She had to crane her neck to take in the strong, angular chin, the firm lips. Holding her breath, she met his blue eyes, and her heart stuttered at the fury they contained.

"You could have been killed! You shouldn't be on a horse if you can't control it. Where are your parents? Surely they don't allow you to ride that horse all over town." His voice boomed, and the crowd that had already gathered grew larger.

Flames of embarrassment licked at her cheeks. He'd chastised her as though she was a child. A child she certainly was not. "I thank you for coming to my rescue. You risked your life to save mine, and there is no way to repay your bravery." She hoped she sounded like one of those rich Southern ladies. People never messed with a Southern lady.

She turned to the other man and blinked, struck by the resemblance to the man who had rescued her. "Thank you kind sir." She raised a hand to make sure her hair was still up and suppressed a groan. Some of the strands still remained secure but most had haphazardly come loose and her tresses had all fallen every which way. *So much for being a fine, Southern lady.*

She gave them both a curt nod and then spun on her heel in the direction she assumed Sunshine went. The crowd was bigger than she'd thought as she made her way through it only to find her Sunshine eating hay out of cart. She marched up to her horse and grabbed the reins. "All this for some hay? Oh, Sunshine how could you? You had plenty of grass to eat, and we've only been away from home a little over a day." Her shoulders slumped as she sighed. She needed a place to repair herself before joining a wagon train and she needed to find one leaving soon.

"Ya'll have to pay for that there hay your horse ate. It's not free you know." A burly man with greasy blond hair approached, and as he came closer she could smell his filth. He had a gleam in his eye she'd seen before and she had no intention of being a victim.

"How much?"

The man smirked as he looked her up and down causing her to shiver. "I'm sure we can work something out."

"How much do you charge for hay? Do you charge by the pitchfork full or cart full?"

His bushy brows came together. "I um, well—"

"It's not your hay, is it?" She put her hands on her hips. If he hadn't had smelled so fowl she would have taken a step forward. "How dare you try to steal money from me! I suggest you leave." She hoped he left before the real owner of the hay came by.

"I'm sure we'll run into each other again soon." He smirked at her again before he turned and walked away. Her stomach clenched at the possibilities of what could have happened with such a lecherous man.

"He gave up easily."

Startled, Susan's heart skipped a beat. She quickly glanced over her shoulder and nodded to the man who'd rescued her. "I never did get your name."

He waited for her to turn in his direction and then he smiled. "I'm Mike Todd. The man you just tangled with is a mean one. You'll want to watch to be sure you're never alone with him."

"Thank you, Mr. Todd, for your advice." She smiled back.

"No thanks needed, ma'am, and it's Mike."

"I'm Susan Farr. It's nice to make your acquaintance. You'll have to excuse my appearance I'm afraid."

He stared into her eyes. "There's nothing wrong with your appearance, Miss Farr."

"Please, call me Susan." She tilted her head a bit. She'd often observed how rich woman acted and it was paying off.

"Fine, Susan. Now where are your parents? Do they know how much trouble you're making in town?" His voice grew deeper.

"My parents passed recently. It's just me and Sunshine. I was hoping to join one of those wagon trains to the west. I've always enjoyed traveling." She batted her eyelashes at him and felt affronted when he laughed.

"Listen lady, this is no vacation. You must be able to work and work hard in order for any wagon master to take you on. Since no one takes women traveling alone, you'll have to rethink your plans."

Dang, I overdid the fine southern lady act. "Mike, I'm quite adept at working hard."

"Doing what? Needlepoint? I'm sorry but I've taken chances with women like you before, and it never ended in a good way. I can't take the time to look after a helpless female and I refuse to break up fights among the men who will try to catch your eye. No. Like I said you need a new plan."

"When are you leaving?"

"You're not listening to a word I have to say." He frowned.

"Oh, I'm listening. When are you leaving?" She tapped her foot.

"In the morning. I wish you luck, Miss Farr. Good bye."

She watched him until he was swallowed up in the distance. She needed a strategy to get on that wagon train and she needed one now.

THE NEXT MORNING, Mike and his brothers Jed and Eli were

all busy helping the members of their party get ready to leave. There were stubborn oxen that needed to be yoked and hitched. Despite earlier instructions, meals were not all done being cooked and it was past time to pack up. A few of the women looked as though they wanted to cry. Children ran all over the place and most didn't heed their parents' calls.

Then there were those who'd been ready right on time griping about the delay. Mike had to bite his lip to keep from laughing. It was always like this the first few days. He rode Arrow up and down the line of wagons giving advice until he came to a wagon closer to the end. His eyes narrowed when he spotted Susan Farr. *Dang it all!*

He guided Arrow to the wagon she was packing. "Miss Farr, I'm surprised to see you here." He hoped his voice conveyed his annoyance.

"Oh hello, Mike. Beautiful day isn't it?" She gave him a quick uncertain smile and went back to loading the wagon.

"I already told you not to come. Why are you here?"

Her shoulders tensed as she turned toward him. "I got married yesterday. I'm not a single woman anymore, and my husband was already part of your party. There's no reason I can't go now is there?"

"Where is your husband?" Her news shocked him.

"Grabbing a few more minutes of sleep."

Mike swung down off his horse and stalked over to the wagon. He took one look inside and shook his head. She'd paired up with a real winner. Clancy Willis was a bit of a drinker. He was hungover, no doubt. "Hey, Clancy!" he yelled into the wagon. "Time to go if you don't want to be left behind." When he received no reply he took a cup filled it with water and threw it at Clancy's head.

Clancy sputtered. "Why'd you have to go and do that?"

"Get up and help your wife! We're ready to leave."

Clancy held his head in his hands. "You don't have to yell so loud. Besides I'm sure Sarah has everything done."

Mike took a deep breath and willed himself not to beat the man. "Susan, her name is Susan. Get up and help her." He muttered under his breath and when he turned around he was tempted to swear. Susan's big blue eyes were filled with panic.

"You won't leave us behind will you?"

"Where's your horse?"

"I gave Sunshine to Clancy to pay for my part of the provisions." Her gaze fell to the ground and her shoulders slumped.

"Just get ready to go. I'll send Jed down to give you a hand but this is a onetime thing. I have to check on the rest of the group. Good day, Susan." He mounted Arrow, tipped his hat and rode off. The money from selling Susan's horse was probably long gone, and Mike had no doubt it had not been spent on provisions. Except for more whiskey, of course. But with fifty wagons and over a hundred people to look out for, that wasn't his problem unless it endangered the wagon train. Susan had made a poor choice, and he was sorry for her.

He sent Jed to help her. She was going to have a hell of a time with a man like Clancy, but it wasn't his business unless it endangered the wagon train. It really was a shame; she was such a pretty little lady with a whole lot of gumption.

Finally both Jed and Eli joined him at the front of the train. It was time to go. "Wagons ho!" Mike yelled, his heart filled with pride as one wagon after another rolled by. The crunch of the wheels on the earth and the plodding sounds of the oxen as they went by lent to a sense of excitement. He could feel it in the air. Most heeded his advice about keeping the wagons light and having everyone but the driver walk. The exception was the Willis wagon. Susan struggled to drive it, but she looked to be giving it her all. Dang, she didn't have a pair of work gloves. The traces were going to make a mess out of her pretty hands. He jolted upright with a little start *pretty hands?* He'd best stay away from Susan her being a married woman. Plus he never became involved with other women. He wasn't in the market, and he didn't trifle with their feelings. One thing he could say about himself, he wasn't a cad.

"Jed, I need you to ride near the back for a while before you go and scout out where to camp. Eli, you take the middle. Remember we have a mixture of greenhorns and farmers. There's bound to be plenty of frustrations until the greenhorns learn the way of things."

"How far did you want to go today?" Jed asked. Of his two brothers, Jed was the most serious of them. "Let's go for ten miles so we can make sure they have plenty of time to figure out a routine for taking care of the livestock, cooking meals and the like."

"Sounds good, I'll go eat some dust at the back of the line for a while." Jed turned his horse and rode to the back part of the train.

"Eli, let me know if any trouble arises."

Eli grinned. "You can count on me, Mike." He too turned his horse and rode away.

Mike reached into his saddle bag and grabbed out two worn bandannas. He rode to the Willis wagon and slowed until he was riding at Susan's side. He reached over and handed her the bandannas. "Wrap these around your hands; they'll help a bit to keep them from being ripped to shreds. Where's Clancy? Never mind, I already know. How many wagons have you driven?"

She tried to put on the cloths without relinquishing her hold on the lines. "I've driven small farm wagons. Nothing this big before, but I'll get the hang of it. You won't have a reason to send us packing."

He stared into her determined eyes. "That was the furthest thing from my mind. I'll check on you later." He tipped his hat to her before he rode off.

SUSAN'S SHOULDERS felt as though they were being pulled right out of her. Her back ached, and she was hungry and thirsty. She called into the wagon a few times to ask for water and leftover biscuits but her *husband* never answered. He was sleeping, and with each turn of the wheel, she grew more and more angry. She'd been a fool to marry him. She'd been so desperate to leave Missouri, she hadn't thought it all through. He promised to never touch her but now what was to stop him? He was her husband and had his right. She'd thought she'd paid her way by allowing him to sell her beloved horse, Sunshine but, that wasn't true.

Sleep had been in short supply last night. As part of their bargain, Clancy was to sleep under the wagon. It hadn't happened that way. Clancy left her to fend for herself while he and a few friends drank most of the night. He'd come crawling into the wagon and scared her. Luckily, he'd passed out, but she had lain in fear he'd wake up at any time and try to consummate the marriage. Perhaps getting drunk was just a way for Clancy to celebrate leaving. He had acted decent enough when he heard of her plight, stepped right up and offered to help her. A marriage of convenience was what they agreed to.

She shrugged her shoulders and planned to make the best of the situation. If only she'd had more time and hadn't had to flee...

"We there yet?" Clancy's gravelly voice wasn't pleasant

sounding and it began to grate on her nerves. "I assume we have many more miles to go. Could you hand me some water and a biscuit?"

"I'm going back to sleep. Besides I ate all the biscuits."

Her stomach rumbled, and her mouth felt drier at the refusal of water. Her face heated. She'd been treated shabbily before but not like this. It was her own fault. She should have brought a canteen and some biscuits up front. Her sigh was loud but she didn't care. Her day just became much harder.

"Mrs. Willis, you look a bit peaked. Can I do anything for you?" Eli asked as he rode up next to her wagon.

"A sip from your canteen would be wonderful. I didn't think to put one up here with me." She smiled as brightly as she could due to the circumstances.

"Sure thing, ma'am." He handed her his canteen and she took a healthy swig.

It felt glorious wetting her parched mouth and flowing down her raspy throat. Mindful not to take too much more, she put the top on and handed it back. "Thank you."

"Any time, ma'am."

"Call me Susan please."

"Take care, Susan." He rode to the next wagon to check on the occupants.

All three brothers favored each other. They all had dark hair, blue eyes and very strong jaws. She bet when Jed and Eli were full grown they too would be well over six feet like their brother Mike. She continued on, her shoulders aching, her arms burning, and her back knotted so hard, she had to grit her teeth against the pain. Soon enough she'd be stronger and the pain wouldn't be so bad.

She did manage a smile for the children who ran and played tag while walking. Some of the women walked in groups, others walked behind their wagons. They all seemed to be a pleasant lot. She couldn't wait to get to know them.

The party was certainly made up of many people. More than she'd imagined. She was bound to find a friend or two.

The day went on, and Clancy never stirred. Hunger pains ate at her and once again she needed some water. The sun overhead became glaring, although there was a cool breeze. Surely they'd be stopping soon, wouldn't they? She'd noticed that Jed had left and rode on ahead of the party a while ago. Mike and Eli rode from the front of the train to the back and back again. Eli always smiled. Mike, however, barely glanced at her. Had she done something to anger him?

She shrugged to dislodge that thought. Right now he was the least of her problems. What was she going to do about Clancy? She didn't trust him to keep his word, not one bit.

She'd made a decision in haste, and now she was sorry, but it couldn't be undone, at least not until they reached Oregon. The plan included an annulment and a cash settlement from the sale of Sunshine. Foolishly, she put herself at that man's mercy.

"Be ready to stop soon," Eli called out to each driver. They were the most joyous words she'd heard all day.

They were shown how to circle the wagons and once she set the break and tied off the lines her shoulders drooped. She wasn't certain she'd be able to climb down off the wagon. Not that she had a choice. She flexed her pained hands a bit. They were still cut up despite the bandannas but it could have been worse. She stood, and a groan escaped her lips. The distance from the wagon seat to the ground seemed much longer than she'd thought. Hitching up her skirts in one hand, she carefully climbed down and walked straight for the water barrel that hung on the side of the wagon. She drank the cool water right from the dipper, swayed and sat down on the ground.

After she gulped down the remaining water she closed her eyes. She needed to get up and unhitch and unyoke the oxen. They needed to be tended to. Then maybe she'd be able to make something to eat. She'd made so many biscuits that morning so they'd have them throughout the day. What had Clancy expected her to eat? She shook her head. She'd best learn how to do everything; she couldn't count on him.

Gingerly, she got to her feet and put the dipper back into the barrel. She put her hands on the small of her back and stretched. First, she unhitched the oxen, trying her hardest not to get caught in the leather traces. The front two were the lead pair for a reason. They were trained and were easily unyoked. It was the next two that gave her problems. It took so much energy but she succeeded. Food was next on the agenda. She'd have to disturb her *husband.* It was about time he got up anyway, the lazy sot. The back side of the wagon dropped down so she could use it to get the food ready. Once she had that unlatched she hesitated before climbing in. The cast iron pot was in ready reach, and she pulled it out. The food was under the false floor in the wagon. Fortunately, she'd put what she needed where she could easily grab it.

Dang, she'd forgotten about making a fire first. Her heart started to beat faster as she became overwhelmed. A moment to herself was what she craved. She stepped to the outer side of the wagon and tried to collect her thoughts. It had been a hard day, and she expected many more of them. Determined to stand on her own two feet, though, she took a deep breath and vowed not to show an ounce of weakness. She rounded the wagon to make the fire, and there was Clancy standing with a jug of whiskey in his hand.

"Where's my supper? What have you been doing with your time? It figures I up and married a lazy one." His eyes were wide and glassy.

She shuddered. He was probably capable of violence. How was it he had been sober when they married and sober when they packed the wagon? Then he took Sunshine to sell.

Dear Lord, did he spend the money on whiskey? Dare she ask?

"Do we have wood for a fire?" she asked calmly.

"That's your job. Now go get some and be quick about it. Those biscuits didn't last long." He sneered at her and pulled a crate out to sit on.

Her lips formed a straight line as she tried to keep from saying something she might regret. Instead, she walked alone toward the wooded area. She had to walk a while before she found any wood on the ground. It looked as though the forest had been picked over by other travelers. It surprised her that she didn't encounter anyone else looking for wood. They'd probably loaded some in their wagons while they were in Independence. She had all she could carry and was relieved when she found her way back out.

She scurried to make the fire and cut up chunks of beef. She added them to the cast iron pot and placed it over the fire. Next she chopped vegetables and added them along with water into the pot. She needed to figure out a routine to make everything quicker and easier.

She sat on the ground near the fire while Clancy drank and laughed to himself. Glancing around, she saw many families, tired but happy, all sitting around their fire eating. Clancy must have noticed too.

"How come everyone else is eatin' and you're just sitting doing nothing? We'll need more wood for breakfast, or didn't you think of that?"

"It's almost dark."

"That's no excuse, go and get more wood. I can stir whatever is in that pot. It sure doesn't smell all that good." He narrowed his eyes as he stared at her.

She stood, gave the stew a quick stir and left. Clancy's voice had obviously carried given the many expressions of surprise and pity on other peoples' faces. If she hadn't had to leave Missouri, she might have just walked back to where they started. Things could be worse, and tired as she was, she'd get the wood, finish dinner and go to bed.

"I thought I saw you come in here," Mike said, causing her to jump.

"I need some more wood. You didn't need to check on me." Her face heated at his expression of concern.

"You drove the whole way?"

She nodded and kept picking up wood. He took the wood from her and carried it as she added more pieces to the pile.

"Where's your husband been this whole time?"

Her heart dropped. "Why ask? You already know he was in the wagon."

Mike stopped and dropped the wood. He reached out and took her hand in his. Gently he unwrapped the blood soaked bandanna. "I'll find some gloves for you. You'll need to keep these wounds clean. Wash the bandannas tonight and hang them. They'll be ready for you to use tomorrow. Clancy plans to drive tomorrow, doesn't he?"

His gentleness was almost too much for her. It took everything inside her not to weep. "I really should get back."

Mike nodded and picked up the pile of wood. They walked in silence, and when they got back to her wagon, Mike dropped the wood at Clancy's feet and then stared him down. "If you need anything else, Mrs. Willis, let me know." He looked to be barely containing his anger. With a quick nod, he spun on his heel and left.

"What did you tell him?" Clancy demanded. He stood and grabbed her arm hurting her.

"I didn't tell him a thing. My life is my business." She pulled her arm out of his grasp and went to gather the bowls and spoons. She ladled out the hearty stew and handed a bowl to Clancy. "Where's the coffee?"

"We have water." She told him softly.

"I want coffee."

She groaned and grabbed the coffee pot and got the coffee ready to put on the fire. Clancy helped himself to another big portion of the stew and her stomach rumbled. There probably wasn't much left. She took her bowl, dismayed to discover she was right, he hadn't left her a full serving. She would have to make due. By the way it stuck to the bottom of the pot, she knew he hadn't stirred it once.

Disgust invaded her being but there was nothing she could do about it. She sat and ate her food, and when the coffee was ready, she poured him a cup but by then he was more interested in his whiskey. She'd save it for the morning.

She put on some water to heat so she could wash the dishes and her bandannas. Once everything was clean she turned toward Clancy. "Good night." She started to climb into the wagon.

"There's been a change in plans. The wagon is more comfortable than the ground. I'll be sleeping in the wagon from now on. You have a choice. You can either sleep with me or sleep under the wagon." His voice boomed, and she was certain everyone in the whole party knew of her shame.

"The ground will be fine. Good night." She went into the wagon and grabbed an oil cloth and a few blankets. All she wanted was to lay her head down and close her eyes. The ground was fine.

CHAPTER TWO

*M*ike made one last sweep of the encampment before he turned in for the night. When he saw Susan sleeping under the wagon his anger knew no bounds. What he wouldn't give to plant his fist in Clancy's face. Unfortunately, there wasn't much he could do. They were married, and the rest was their business. That was just the way of things. Sometimes there just wasn't anything he could do, and this was one of them. It didn't sit right with him.

He'd make sure Clancy had his share of guard duty and hunting. What kind of man treated a woman the way he treated Susan? She sure tried to put on a brave front, but for some reason he could almost see inside her heart and it was in great pain today. Not from any love of Clancy, but from the disappointment and hardship the day had brought.

He'd find her some gloves to wear in the morning.

Morning always started at four o'clock, when Mike would be up and walking from wagon to wagon seeing who needed help. It was interesting to see who the firemaker in each family was. Some of the men did it for their wives, a few wives did it themselves. He moved on and checked on everyone before he sat down at the supply wagon he had provided for him and his brothers and the driver, Smitty. Smitty was a good guy. His tan, leathered face told a story of too many years in the saddle. They'd known him all their lives. He made sure they were all fed and if they got ill, he fussed over them like an old woman. He'd made the trek west and back many times and they considered him to be family. Plus he was darn good with a gun.

Coffee and food were exactly what Mike needed. He enjoyed this time of day when he, his brothers, and Smitty were able to catch up and alert the others to potential problems. With so many people there were bound to be misunderstandings. It was early days yet. When people began to feel a bit of hopelessness, that they were never going to reach Oregon, tempers usually flared. Mike liked the early days.

"Did you get everyone scheduled for guard duty?" Mike asked Eli.

Eli nodded while he finished chewing the food in his mouth. "Most of them anyway. You know how it is, a few don't know how to shoot a rifle, and then there was that Willis fellow. He claims he's not up to it. He says he's sick, but he smelled like whiskey. I heard he just married that nice woman, Susan. He wouldn't have lasted a day without her. He hasn't lifted a finger as far as I know."

Jed frowned. "Why do people think they can get there without doing the work? I do have to say the majority of our party is made up of sturdy, hardworking people. There are a few hot heads, but we'll deal with them if need be."

Smitty refilled all the coffee cups. "Your folks would have been proud of you boys." He sighed. "Who has guard duty tonight?"

Eli explained the schedule. They split it into two shifts. The shift change was around midnight. "I put some of the greener guys on the early shift. I'll make the rounds to teach them. The second shift I have more seasoned men. I'll explain what they are to do and then I'll grab some shut eye." Eli stood and then grabbed his rifle.

Mike nodded. Smitty was right, their parents would have been proud of all of them. "Have a good night and be careful out there." He watched until Eli was out of sight. He wondered if Susan was making her fire. He needed to keep his head clear of her. She was married, and it would lead to no good.

He stopped and greeted most of the people. He wished he could skip Susan's but the pull to check on her was too strong besides he'd found some gloves for her. She smiled as he approached and her smile went right to his heart. "Good morning."

"Good morning, Mike. Would you like a cup of coffee?"

"We barely have enough for ourselves!" Clancy yelled from inside the wagon.

Mike pretended for her sake he hadn't heard her husband. "I wish I could but I have many more wagons to visit." He started to walk away and then he turned back, drawing a pair of leather gloves out of his back pocket. "I found these for you. You'll be hurting for a few days to come, but they should protect you from further injury."

"Oh, thank you." She took the gloves and her eyes grew wide as she stroked the soft leather. "I appreciate your kindness."

After he tipped his hat, he walked on. It was worth it to see the smile she'd bestowed him. He was already a goner, and he had a big heartbreak in the making, but he couldn't seem to help himself.

HE WALKED to the next wagon and the kindly Mrs. Mott

pulled him to the side. "We need to do something about Mr. Willis. He's a mean one, and she's a brand new bride. Why my heart goes out to her."

"Savanna, I already tol' you it's not our business," her husband Clarke said.

"But surely…" She sighed and wiped a few wisps of her white hair off her forehead.

"Your husband is right, Savanna. Let me know if things get out of hand."

"I will, Mike. It's just so hard to hear and to watch." Savanna smiled at him. "You're a good man, Mike."

"Thank you, Savanna. I'd best get moving on."

THE CAMP BEGAN to stir in the predawn hours, and Susan wished she'd scouted the area she had slept on for rocks before she went to bed. It'd been less than a restful sleep, but she got through the first day, she'd do the same for today. She'd always admired those who showed fortitude, and she planned to do her best to do the same.

She crawled out from under the wagon, gathered up her bedding and folded it. Then she went about her chores as well as she could while she did her best not to wake Clancy. He had gone somewhere last night and fallen a few times getting into the wagon. How could she have been blind to his coarseness? The words he'd used when he fell heated her face, and she had appreciated the darkness.

She filled her canteen and put it up front on the wagon seat. She also made extra biscuits and put her share next to her canteen. Next she filled a pot with water to soak the beans so they'd be ready to cook come nightfall. She wished she'd thought to grab clean clothes last night but she'd just have to wear what she had on. Not that it mattered much.

"There's a creek nearby if you need to top off your water barrel," Jed called to her as he rode past. She nodded her appreciation.

At least she'd be able to wash. Grabbing a bucket, she headed in the direction of the creek. Other members of the party were coming back from it all looking clean. She'd heard there would be times they wouldn't have extra water to wash with. At the banks of the creek, she knelt and splashed water on her face. The cool liquid soothed her battered hands, and she soaked them for a time. She filled her bucket and began to walk back to the camp when a big bear of a man came into view. A full, unkempt beard the color of midnight blended into a mane of thick, loose hair that hung past his shoulders. A shiver rippled through her. The way he ogled her was disconcerting, and she tried to pretend she didn't notice.

He licked his lips as he got closer, and then he smiled. "I was hoping to catch a moment alone with you. You sure are a sweet little thing. I wanted to get a better look before I took your husband up on any of his offers."

Her jaw dropped and her heart beat faster. "What—what offers?"

"I mentioned by the amount he was drinking he'd run dry before much longer. I have a wagon almost filled with the finest whiskey. I'm opening a bar in Oregon. He said if it came to it he'd trade you for a few bottles." His laugh was cruel. He stroked his beard and he seemed to be waiting for an answer.

"Good day." She ran past him.

"The name is Bart, Bart Bigalow! We'll get to know each other at another time then." He laughed again, and it made her skin crawl.

Fear clutched at her chest as she hurried back to her wagon. So much water had sloshed out of the bucket there wasn't very much left to put in the barrel. She poured it in anyway and heard a snicker from inside the wagon.

"Can't do anything right, can ya? You need to fill the bucket up when you're at the water."

Susan ignored Clancy and went about packing the wagon. If she was too loud, Clancy moaned and told her to stop making noise if she knew what was good for her. She'd be just as glad if he just slept all day again. It was easier than listening to him.

She began to shovel dirt on the now dying fire when she heard the sound of water. Turning around she was surprised to see Mike filling her barrel. His simple act of kindness made her want to cry.

"Thank you," she said her voice heavy.

"I'm here to help." He grinned at her and then walked to the Motts' wagon. They looked like good people. Perhaps she'd get a chance to know them soon.

"If you can't do the work right, you'll get us kicked off," Clancy warned.

"You're welcome to help me." She put her hand over her mouth. He was bound to be angry with her. She quickly went to gather their oxen, chastising herself the whole time. She needed a knife or something to carry, and she'd best tread lightly.

Horses she was used to. Oxen seemed almost intimidating but she could do it. She had to do it, and her hope was they'd cooperate. They were happy enough to be unhitched last night. Before she even had a chance to try, Eli rode up, jumped off his horse and had the four oxen gathered.

"I do know how," she said hoping she hadn't looked helpless.

"I know you do. I saw you yesterday. You handled them quite well. I just thought I'd give you a hand is all. How are your hands by the way?" He stared at her gloves.

"Thanks to your brother, I'll be just fine. I wasn't as prepared as I should have been for the trip." She gave him a slight smile. It was better to make light of things.

Eli grinned. "Everyone forgets something." He quickly and skillfully yoked and hitched the oxen and then tied the lines around the brake. "Off to see who else I can help."

"Thank you, Eli."

He nodded, mounted his horse, and rode off.

"You like them young, don't ya?" Clancy slurred as he rounded to the front of the wagon. "What did you tell him? Did you tell him I couldn't handle the animals?"

A shiver of fear ran up her spine. "Of course not. I wouldn't speak ill of you. You're my husband."

The menace in his eyes lessened. "I'm going to sleep for a while. Take a care when driving. You drove over too many dang bumps yesterday."

She watched him climb back into the wagon and frowned. He'd been such a different person when he was sober. His willingness to help her out had impressed her, and she'd been confident they'd get on. Unfortunately she'd been terribly wrong.

Her shoulders and arms ached, but she climbed up onto the wagon seat and waited for the signal for them to move out.

Looking down at her gloves, she smiled. At least someone cared, even if was just a little bit. The wagon in front of her began to pull out. She waited a few breaths and then urged her oxen forward. The wagon lurched forward. They were on their way again. She held the lines and steadily drove the wagon until the noon break. This time she had her own biscuits to eat. She unhitched the oxen, rubbed them down with a bit of hay, and led them to water before she found herself a rock to sit on. There was no sense in peeking in the wagon. She didn't want to disturb Clancy. She sighed as she unwrapped her biscuits.

She'd learn to do it all on her own. Clancy had been a means to get on the wagon train. He'd served his purpose. Bart Bigalow could send her all the snide looks he wanted. His threat of Clancy trading her to him for whiskey was just an empty threat. No one they were traveling with would stand for it.

Pushing to her feet, she stretched her neck one way then the next then raised her arms over head trying to lessen her tight muscles. Hard work never scared her and she was up for the challenge. She wondered if the banker, Mr. Benton had found Sunshine yet. When he'd given her the eviction notice, he had warned her to not take one single thing from the property—only her clothes.

Her heart squeezed painfully. Losing her Pa had been so unexpected. *Dang that Mr. Benton.* He'd driven his buggy out to her land the same day as the funeral and told her to vacate. She left that very night taking her horse Sunshine and her ma's silver candlesticks. She'd even left all the stall doors open, and the barn door. He'd have a time finding the horses and cow.

She'd been tempted for a moment to burn down the house but in the end her conscience wouldn't allow it. Her pa had taken out a loan against the farm. It was one of the hardest things she'd ever done, leaving the farm, but she couldn't stay. Her father's body wasn't even cold before she'd had one offer to be a man's mistress. She'd rather die than go against the teachings of her family.

"You look lost in thought." She jumped at Mike's deep voice.

"You caught me." She smiled at him. "What's your horse's name?" She'd admired the big bay horse.

"His name is Arrow. We've traveled many miles together." He raised his left brow. "Is everything fine here?"

She blushed and glanced away for a moment. *He knew.* "Never better." She hoped her smile looked genuine. Looking into his blue eyes, she realized she'd failed. There was a hint of anger in them.

"Where's your husband?" Mike's voice sounded almost harsh.

"He's not feeling well. He's lying down." She wanted to look away again but he held her gaze. His anger turned into concern and it warmed her a bit. She wasn't completely alone after all. "I can handle things."

"I know you can. I'll check back later." He touched the brim of his hat and rode to the wagon behind her.

She grinned. He had no idea how handsome he was. He'd make someone a fine husband one day.

CHAPTER THREE

*T*he Blue River lay ahead and Mike gave the signal for them to stop early. The first crossing was always a bit difficult. The animals and their owners were all inexperienced and nervous. He'd need to go over with each driver what needed to be done. They'd have to ford the river if it wasn't too high. He'd sent Eli ahead to check, and when he spotted his brother heading their way, he spurred Arrow on to meet him.

"It's the lowest I've seen it this time of year. We'll make it across no problem." Eli smiled. "I haven't seen other wagons either."

"It's a gamble leaving early in the year. We still have plenty of time for bad conditions. Let's get this first set of wagons going, and we'll have Jed explain to the rest what they are to do." Mike smiled, encouraged by the good news. Plenty of times they'd had to wait days for the river to go down enough to cross.

Just as he predicted, there was an air of unease during the crossing. Compared to many, this one was going to be easy. He and Eli rode their horses back and forth helping each wagon across. When it was Susan's turn, he swallowed hard. Her face was so very white and her eyes appeared bigger than usual. He bet her knuckles were white under her gloves.

"I'll drive it across for you," he offered.

She shook her head. "You haven't had to drive anyone else's, and you won't need to start with mine. I can do this." She pursed her lips in a particularly stubborn way. Even with her lips drawn up so tight, she was beautiful.

"Fine, we'll go straight across. Do not stop for any reason. I'll be on one side of the wagon and Eli will be on the other side." He waited for her to nod. "Let's get you across."

She drove the wagon into the river and straight to the other side. Mike was proud of her gumption. She did what she had to. He gave her a smile and went back across to help the next wagon.

They'd been at it all afternoon and were close to finishing when a mother frantically screamed. Her child had fallen into the river. Mike also heard the child yell and he tried to pinpoint where she was. He spotted the tiny form being carried away in the rushing water.

The driver started to turn the wagon and almost knocked Mike off his horse. Thankfully, Eli grabbed the lines and pulled the oxen and wagon out of Mike's way. Mike spurred Arrow up the riverbank and he rode like the very devil was after him trying to spot the girl. He'd lost sight of her.

He rode up and down the bank until he could see the girl's head bobbing up and down. He rode back into the cold river and reached down into the water. *Damn he missed.* He reached out again and this time he caught hold of her arm. He lifted her up in front of him when he saw the driver wash by with his face covered in blood. Eli raced to them and took the girl from Mike.

"Her pa dove in and a log slammed into his head," Eli yelled.

Mike rode farther down the river but couldn't quite catch up with the fast current? The last glimpse he saw of the man's sightless eyes and limp body confirmed what he'd already thought. The man was dead. It was a bitter pill to swallow. These people were in his care, and he knew they'd lose a few—they always did—but it always felt like a huge blow. Now the horrible task of telling the poor man's family there was no body to bury.

Someone had made a big fire, and the shivering girl and her mother were huddled in front of it. The hope in their eyes quickly dimmed as he shook his head. His heart squeezed as Mrs. Lewis threw back her head and wailed. Poor Lily sat silently beside her all soaking wet. He watched as Jed placed a blanket around the girl.

There was nothing worse than feeling helpless, nothing at all. It ate at him when senseless things like this happened. Ever since he'd had to take responsibility for his brothers, his gut twisted and his heart raced when he wasn't in control. Mike took a deep breath and let it out slowly. He was well aware that the whole company was looking to him to lead them.

"Can someone help Lily into some dry clothes?" he asked and was pleased when Mrs. Mott helped Lily up and led her to the Lewis' wagon. "We'll camp here for the night. It's been an exhausting day." He wished he had words of wisdom to bestow but there was nothing he could say to comfort Mrs. Lewis.

As he walked through the crowd, plenty of people patted him on the back for saving Lily, but it didn't make him feel any better. It was times like this he wished he could pour himself some whiskey, but he needed a clear head at all times.

Susan had already done most of the chores and she had dinner simmering in a cast iron pot. She couldn't help but glance in the direction of the Lewis wagon. Many of the group surrounded it, lending support to the family. She wished she could go too, but she wasn't sure if it was her place. Clancy might object. Her heart hurt, and loneliness engulfed her. She still mourned the loss of her parents, and she knew the hell of being told a loved one was no longer.

Sitting on an empty crate, she stirred her stew and despite the warmth of the fire, she shivered.

"Are you alright?" Mike's voice startled her.

"You're always sneaking up on me." She tried to smile but stopped. Now wasn't the time for smiles.

"It's hard losing one of our party. Have no illusions there will be more, I just wish..." He shook his head and swallowed hard. She watched his Adam's apple move up and down.

She tilted her head and met his gaze. "You did what you could at considerable risk to yourself. You managed to save Lily. You're right, it is hard to lose someone. But none of us is immune to the ways of the world. We never seem to know what might happen." She sighed. "Will we be continuing on tomorrow?"

"We'll have to. It looks like it may rain tonight, and we want to make sure we aren't stuck in the mud. It makes for some hard going, but it's better to keep moving when we can. Tell Clancy he'll be expected to help move the wagons tomorrow. We'll need everyone's strong backs."

Clancy climbed out of the wagon. He gave them both thunderous looks while he scratched his belly. "I have oxen for that. Don't count me in." He walked past Susan and practically upended her. If she hadn't been quick on her feet, she'd have been charred.

"Is dinner ready? I'm starved. What's all that caterwauling

about?" He turned to Mike. "You're in charge. Can't you do something about that noise?"

Susan cringed at her husband's words. "Mr. Lewis died today as we crossed the river."

"We all got to go sometime. This isn't going to hold us up, is it? We have a long ways to go, and we need to push on." He frowned as he shook his head.

"We're pushing on all right, and that's why we need your help. We'll be mired in mud come morning, and everyone will have to help push the wagons. Have a nice night." Mike touched the brim of his hat and nodded to her and then he frowned at Clancy before walking away.

"He needs to show me a little more respect," Clancy huffed.

"He has a lot on his mind, I suppose." She hurried and ladled out the stew to keep Clancy quiet. It would only be a momentary silence, but she'd take what she could get. Once seated again, she glanced up at the sky. Angry dark clouds were indeed rolling in. The scent of impending rain swept through the camp.

It wasn't very dark yet, but she needed to secure her bed under the wagon before the ground became too wet. She left her seat at the fire and grabbed her bedroll along with an extra oil cloth. She'd need the usual one under her and the additional one on top of her. The last few mornings she'd woken up to her blanket damp from the morning dew. It hadn't bothered her but the storm might. Lightning scared her something awful. What a predicament but no matter what she refused to sleep in the wagon with her so-called husband.

Mrs. Mott hurried over to her. "Dear, you can't sleep on the ground tonight. You'll make yourself sick." Her motherly smile and snow-white hair brought a sense of peace.

"Thank you for your concern, Mrs. Mott—"

"Call me Savanna. It's not my place to speak ill of anyone but if you need to take cover we're right here. Oh, and Susan, you might want to make extra food tonight. It may be too wet to start a fire in the morning. I always set aside extra biscuits, and my Clarke will drink coffee cold."

"You're so very thoughtful. I think I'll take your advice about the food. I hadn't thought about it. Thank you." Susan smiled. She'd made a friend.

THE WIND KICKED UP, and Mike, Jed, and Eli went from wagon to wagon, helping the settlers to secure their canvases onto their wagons. He'd advised them earlier to do it, but almost half of the wagons needed retying. It was part of the job. He glanced at the Willis wagon and was glad to see it secured. The rain poured down in sheets, and instantly it became difficult to see. The thunder boomed loudly, and the lightning lit up the sky. Fortunately, the lightning wasn't striking anywhere near them.

He yelled for Jed and Eli to get back to the wagon and out of the torrential weather. Meanwhile, he made one more slow sweep of the circle. He'd hear a scream here and there in reaction to the lightning and thunder. There was weeping in the Lewis wagon, but that was understandable. The ground had soaked up all that it could and the rain began to form big puddles. It was going to be a mess in the morning.

As he walked by the Mott wagon, Clarke Mott stuck his head out and asked him to check on Susan. Mike's stomach dropped. Certainly, she wasn't under the wagon. He only had to take a few steps to see that she was indeed huddled on the ground. Her attempts to keep dry looked to be futile.

He squatted down and tried to talk to her, but the storm raged on, making hearing hard. He made a quick decision and crawled under the wagon with her. Her body shook, and she cringed with each boom. "What are you doing out here?" He asked right into her ear. He was so close he could smell the lavender scent she wore.

She turned and stared at him. They lay face to face, and he could feel her breath on his cheek. Glancing at her lips was a mistake. They were ripe and somehow enticing, and he needed to keep his distance.

"I'm trying to sleep!" she yelled over the wind.

"Come with me before you drown." He didn't wait for an answer, just scooted out from under the wagon and pulled her with him. Next, he scooped her up into his arms. Even wet, she hardly weighed much. He walked toward the back of her wagon, but she started to fight him. He quickly turned in the other direction and deposited her just inside of the Mott's wagon.

"Hope this is fine with you!" He yelled to Clarke.

Savanna already had Susan wrapped in a quilt before Clarke could answer. Seeing she was safe, Mike left. *Foolish woman*. His lips tugged upwards. She sure had grit, though. She made him feel... He frowned as he thought of her husband. She was Clancy's responsibility, and he had no right to interfere.

After a final glance through the rain revealed no obvious problems, Mike made his way to his wagon. As he climbed inside, he discovered Eli, Jed, and Smitty were all still awake. "We'd best get some shut eye," he said as he shucked his wet clothes. "We're going to be busy pushing wagons tomorrow."

The next morning was just as Mike had predicted. The wagon wheels were sitting deep in mud. Most folks didn't bother trying to make a morning fire. Smitty, however, did make one and invited people to use it to make coffee. He was a generous soul.

As people gathered by the Todd wagon, many opinions

on how to proceed were made known. Almost all of them didn't involve the men pushing the wagons.

"Some great ideas, but here's what we are going to do. The woman or boy in your party will drive while the men get behind the wagon and push."

"Now see here!" said a stocky man with blond hair and a fancy jacket he pushed his way to the front of the crowd. "I don't plan on pushing anyone else's wagon. Just my own. I'll not tire myself out."

Elton Sugarton had been a thorn in Mike's side from the beginning. He always complained and if he wasn't doing so, then his wife Trudy was. Mike took his hat off and raked his fingers through his hair.

"Listen up everyone! We will help one another. Those who don't will be left behind."

Elton frowned. "The animals are supposed to pull the wagon. I don't understand why we don't just hitch a few extra oxen to each wagon and get it going."

"I'm captain of this party, and what I say goes but I'll explain it to you. Once a wagon is moving, it has to stay moving or it will become stuck again as soon as we stop and we'd have to start over again. We'll be pushing wagons all day as it is. They will get stuck again, but I'm hoping we can get in as many miles as possible."

"Tomorrow is Sunday," Trudy said. Her blond hair was unbound and blowing in the wind. "We'll have a day of rest of course." She smiled. Mike couldn't tell but it looked like a smug smile to him.

Mike held up his hand quieting the crowd. "I know a lot of you are used to church on Sunday, but out here if the weather is good we travel. We can stop an hour early tomorrow to give the folks who want to get together and worship time to do so."

Most people nodded but not the Sugar Tons. They both

glared at him. He shrugged. He was there to lead not to make friends. "I'm putting the Lewis wagon in the front today. He glanced at the Mott's it had been their turn to be first, but they didn't even blink. They just nodded. Susan stood with them. She wore something entirely too big on her. Probably something of Savanna Mott's. He scanned the rest of the crowd, but there was no sign of Clancy.

Enough was enough, he was going to pour out his stash of whiskey if that was what it took for him to show up to meetings and for him to pull his weight. Perhaps he'd be kinder to his wife, not that it was any of his business.

As he strode to the Willis wagon, he felt Susan's wide eyed gaze on him. Clancy wasn't going to get special treatment. He stopped at the tailgate and yelled for Clancy. It took a minute or so, but Clancy showed his head out the back of the wagon.

"What do you want?" Clancy's eyes were bloodshot.

"I told you yesterday that you were needed to push wagons out of the mud."

Clancy laughed. "I'm not feeling that well. Ask my wife. I've been poorly lately."

"Drinking whiskey all day will do that to you. Did you even bother to check on your wife last night? That was a powerful storm we had." Mike crossed his arms in front of him and stared right back at Clancy.

"She's fine. No need for you to bother yourself with her."

"Get up, and get out here. We have work to do. Yours is the third wagon, and we don't need the extra weight of you in it."

"You can't—" Mike reached in and grabbed Clancy by the scruff of his neck and pulled him out of the wagon.

"Yes I can." He glanced around, ignoring the onlookers, until he saw Susan. "You can get dressed now in peace. We'll be pushing you out in a few minutes."

Susan stepped forward and without looking at either him or Clancy, climbed into the back of the wagon.

"Come on, Clancy, we have the Lewis wagon to start with." Mike didn't wait. He walked on to the wagon, satisfied with the amount of men willing to help. "This will be dirty work, fellas, but we can do it and when they get stuck again, we'll do it all over again."

Soon they had the Lewis wagon and the Motts' on their way. Next up was Susan, and he wouldn't have believed it if he hadn't seen it, but quick as lightening Clancy climbed up onto the wagon bench. He tried to wrestle the lines from Susan who seemed to be holding on for all she was worth. When that didn't work he gave her a shove off the seat. She almost went tumbling to the ground but she managed to hold onto the side of the wagon and stay in her seat.

"Hold up! Clancy get down from there and get your sorry behind back here and push. I'm out of patience with you."

"Doesn't matter to me how you feel. You have it out for me," Clancy griped.

Mike would have to talk to Susan later. Clancy's insolence couldn't go unchallenged. He either needed to change his attitude or leave the wagon party. It wasn't a talk Mike was looking forward to.

CHAPTER FOUR

*E*xhausted, beyond exhausted, barely able to move, were words that came to Susan's mind. It had been a wet miserable day of listening to Clancy constantly whine. All day he complained and called Mike and his brothers names behind their backs. Every chance he got he pulled her down off the driver's seat and took the seat for himself, telling her to walk.

She didn't mind the walking except for the mud trying to suck her shoes right off her feet. Mike, Eli, and Jed all minded. Clancy wasn't available to help push wagons out of the mud if he was driving. There were men who had to drive, they didn't have anyone else who could take over. She'd heard about each of them again and again from Clancy. Frankly, she was fed up with him but she wasn't in a position to set him right.

It was slow going but she did get a chance to visit with Savanna Mott while she walked beside the Mott wagon. Savanna was a lovely woman with good common sense. She too agreed that Susan was stuck in her pretend marriage until they reached Oregon. She also cautioned her to never be alone with him in case he decided to make the marriage real. So much easier said than done, but she'd be on her guard.

Finally, Mike called out for them to circle the wagons. All she wanted to do was lie down and sleep, but the chores needed to be done, and Clancy would be of no help. How could she have misjudged him by so much? He had been such a different man in Independence. But there was no going back now. Susan caught up to her wagon, and discovered the oxen were still hitched. It wasn't a surprise, but her shoulders slumped all the same.

Slowly, she unhitched the lines, unyoked them and rubbed them down. Oxen were important. Without them, they'd never make it to Oregon. She wished she had time to check in on Natalie and Lily Lewis. How awful for them to have to go on without Mr. Lewis. But there simply wasn't time for such calls today.

Using some wood she had stashed in the wagon to keep it dry, she built their fire and started supper, including a couple extra batches of biscuits.

Clancy had disappeared, and the quiet was a nice change. The way he'd treated her all day had been humiliating. She would bet she was the topic of conversation around many campfires tonight. Her face heated just thinking about it. Slowly, she turned her head this way and that to see the others and yes, she was being talked about. There were looks of pity but the laughter was the hardest to take. Why were some people just plain mean?

The worst was a pretty woman named Connie. She had striking blond hair and green eyes, and she believed herself to be the envy of all women. She traveled with her father who everyone called Ranger. He was a decent enough fella, but his daughter flirted to no end with every man, married or not. Surprisingly, Connie had a group of friends. None of the married women wanted anything to do with her, but almost everyone's daughter seemed to adore her.

Connie sat on a stool surrounded by her friends, and they all erupted in laughter. Susan glanced their way and found them all staring at her. Several whispered behind their hands. All she could do was turn away. She'd grown up to be generous of spirit and didn't understand people like Connie. Life was too hard, trying to survive and keep food on the table. Susan never had the luxury of gossiping nor did she want to.

"Hello." Mike's voice came from next to her.

She stood and shook her head. "You have to stop sneaking up on me." She tried to smile but was too tired.

"I have to search your wagon."

"Whatever for?" She frowned and tilted her head.

He took a step closer to her. "I need to find all the whiskey and pour it out. I don't allow drunkenness on the trail. I've looked the other way where Clancy was concerned, and it wasn't right. It's a dangerous enough trip without having a drunkard with us. He didn't seem like a drinking man when he signed up."

"I thought the same when I married him. He'll be angry." She clasped her hands in front of her. Clancy was sure to trade her to Bart for more whiskey.

"I'll deal with him. Right now, I need to get rid of the liquor."

"I understand." She watched as he climbed into the wagon. Her hands shook as she thought of the consequences she'd face. Mike was doing his job, but it put her in a hard place.

A few minutes later, he exited the wagon with six full bottles and one half-full bottle in his arms. "Where is Clancy?"

"I don't know. By the time I caught up to the wagon, he'd

left. The oxen were still hitched, but he was gone." She took a deep breath. It was going to be one terrifying night.

"I'll stick close so I can talk to him when he returns." He started to walk away but turned back toward her. "I'm sorry about this."

"He was so different, I don't know what happened." She couldn't take the compassion in his eyes any longer. She stared at the ground instead.

"I'll get rid of these. Don't worry."

Her pride was in tatters. Everyone felt pity for her, except for those who laughed. She'd felt alone plenty of times lately, but this time she felt more alone than ever. Clancy would be furious, and she'd pay the price.

Sure enough, after dark, Clancy came stumbling toward the fire.

"Where were you?" she asked.

"Well, my pretty wife, there's another wagon party not far from us. Got a ride with Ole Bart. We had a high old time."

"You're drunk again," she hissed.

"Of course I am. They had a wagon filled with whores. These ladies were mighty fine and worth every cent." He winked at her.

She shuddered. His voice was so loud the whole camp probably heard him. "Keep your voice down."

"Why? You don't want the good people to know you won't allow me to touch you? They might not like the fact that you're not doing your duty toward your husband. You are a poor excuse for a wife," he bellowed, his face growing mottled.

Mike appeared out of the darkness. "Susan, grab whatever you need for the night. The Mott's have offered you a place to stay the night. Clancy, I suggest you sleep it off. We'll talk in the morning."

"You just want to steal my wife. You can have her." He

grabbed Susan's arm and shoved her toward Mike. "Now she belongs to you. Nature calls and she'd best have all of her things out of my wagon before I get back!" He stumbled off into the darkness.

She felt the blood drain from her face. She had the Mott's for the night but after that, she had nowhere to go. She'd given Clancy all her money. Maybe she could ask for it back.

"Susan?" Mike reached out and touched her arm. "Let's get you packed while we can."

Tears trailed down her face. "Yes, of course." She climbed into the wagon but she couldn't think. Her mind was jumbled full of what would happen to her. The wagon tipped a bit as Mike climbed in beside her.

"Do you have a bag?"

She stared at him then blinked. "Yes, Yes I do and we can put my things in it. I don't have much." She took her clothes, her bible and everything else she'd come to independence with. She also took a bedroll and extra blankets.

Mike raised one brow. "Is that all?"

"Things aren't that important. After all you can only wear one dress at a time." She took a deep breath and let it out slowly. "I'm ready to go."

Mike grabbed a canteen and put it in the bag before he dropped it out of the wagon. After jumping out he turned back with his arms outstretched for her. She could sense the strength of him as he put his hands around her waist and swung her through the air until she was gently set on her feet. It was curious how he made her so warm and tingly just by being near her. She didn't understand it. After he set her down, grabbed her bag and offered her his arm. He escorted her to the Mott's who were so very kind, it made her cry in earnest.

"Take care of her for me. Clancy doesn't know I took his

whiskey yet. Jed will sleep under your wagon tonight. I have a feeling Clancy won't be happy."

Clarke Mott shook Mike's hand. "Don't you worry. She's in good hands."

Mike smiled at her. "Things will be better tomorrow. Get some sleep alright?"

Not trusting her voice, Susan nodded and wiped her eyes with a handkerchief Savanna Mott handed to her.

IT WAS NO USE, he wouldn't find sleep. Mike tossed and turned under his wagon, and when he heard Smitty get up before dawn, he followed and laid the fire. Smitty nodded his thanks and put the coffee on to boil.

"You didn't sleep a wink," Smitty said.

"I look that bad?"

"No, Mike, I heard you all night long. Snoring doesn't bother me. Sometimes there's a rhythm to it, but tossing and grunting when you roll on a rock, that disturbs my sleep."

"I'm sorry."

"It's fine. Want to talk about it?" Smitty went to the back of the wagon and folded the wooden tailgate down to use as a place to prepare food.

"There's really not much to talk about. Clancy is going to blow when he finds his liquor gone. I'm worried about him taking it out on Susan."

"His wife."

"Yes, Smitty, his wife. I know better than to interfere, but I won't allow him to harm her. Dang it, I feel responsible for her. I told her she couldn't join us unless she was married." He heard a gasp behind him and he stiffened and turned.

"I'm not your responsibility. I knew what I was doing

when I got married, and you're right, you shouldn't interfere. I stopped by to say thank you. Good day."

He watched her walk away. She'd looked regal standing there with the wind whipping through her hair and a look of determination on her face. Under it all, he sensed a bit of hurt mixed in with her anger.

Smitty crossed his arms in front of him. "Well?"

"Well, what?"

"Dang it, Mike, go after the gal. Clancy is bound to find out about his whiskey soon."

Mike nodded and jammed on his hat. "I'll be back. Save me some food."

"Don't I always?"

Mike smiled as he walked away. He could always count on Smitty.

A roar of anger could be heard throughout the camp, and Mike picked up his pace. Clancy must have found out about his missing bottles. His long strides became a sprint when he spotted Jed holding Clancy back from the Mott's wagon. Intense body odor mixed with liquor and a faint trace of perfume assaulted Mike as he grasped Clancy by his filthy shirt. Together, he and Jed dragged the unkempt man to his wagon.

Mike unceremoniously shoved him to the ground and towered over him. "If you're looking for your whiskey, you won't find it. I poured it out last night. I warned you about your drinking. I don't tolerate drunkards on the trail. You're a danger to yourself and to the rest of us. I expect you to pull your weight or you're welcome to leave."

Clancy's eyes narrowed as he stared at Mike. "You'd like that wouldn't you? You'd just love to have my wife all to yourself. Don't think I haven't seen how you stare at her and how she stares right back at you. I'm continuing on, but Susan is no longer welcome in my wagon."

There was a gasp from the crowd that had gathered. Many looked at Clancy in disgust but there were enough people who looked at Mike in the same way. *Damn.* He needed their confidence and their respect in order to be an effective leader. He glanced over at Susan. She looked frail standing there alone with her face so very pale and drawn. He had to struggle against his instinct to go to her and reassure her.

"If you plan on traveling with us there will be no more drinking. You will take your assigned turn at guard duty. You will drive your own wagon and take care of your oxen. Think of this is your second and last chance. Do we understand each other?"

Clancy stood and spit on the ground. "Understood." He turned and climbed into the back of his wagon.

Mike turned to the crowd. "Nothing more to see here folks. Might as well get ready to move out." He stood and stared at them until the last of the stragglers left. What to do about Susan? The Motts had been very kind to her but he didn't think they were in a position to take on an extra person to feed. He found himself glancing everywhere except for where Susan stood. Perhaps the Lewises could take her in their wagon. She'd be an asset to them, and Lord knew they needed all the help they could get.

Mike walked to the Lewis wagon and chatted with Mrs. Lewis. His heart lightened when she agreed to take Susan in. He thanked her, and as he walked back to the Motts' wagon he sighed in relief. Hopefully that would take care of the problem for today. On his way to get Arrow, he waved Eli over.

"Do me a favor and make sure Susan get settled in at the Lewis wagon. I also want the line order changed up. Let's put the Lewis wagon behind the Motts and move Clancy's wagon back to where the Lewis wagon was. A little distance might help." He smiled at Eli and then went on to find Arrow. After saddling and mounting his horse, he rode to the beginning of the train and yelled out, "Wagons ho!"

It took everything he had to keep from checking on Susan throughout the day, but he didn't want any more tongues wagging. Susan was a sweet, kind woman, and she didn't deserve to be gossiped about. He figured if he kept his eye on Clancy that should be good enough.

The mud wasn't as bad as the day before, but a few of the wagons did get stuck. This time the settlers knew what to do and they got started again fairly quickly. Upon stopping for the noon meal, he was approached by the Sugartons. He wanted to groan when he saw Trudy and Elton hurrying toward him.

After greeting them with a nod, Mike waited for them to speak. He knew it had something to do with Susan, and he really wasn't in the mood.

Trudy Sugarton put her hands on her hips and pursed her lips as she stared at him. Finally, she opened her mouth. "We don't think it's right the way you changed up the order of the wagons. Why should the Lewis wagon be up front? Is it because Mr. Lewis is dead or is it because Susan is now riding with them?"

Elton stood by his wife and nodded.

Mike crossed his arms in front of him and took his time in answering. "It's more of a safety concern than favoritism. You're right, Mrs. Lewis did lose her husband and she really doesn't know how to drive her wagon very well. You're also right that Susan is now riding in the Lewis wagon. Usually I don't take the time to explain my decisions, but since you asked so nicely that's my answer."

"See, Elton, I told you it was favoritism. Everyone else has to take turns but not the Lewises. Now, what about the Motts? Will they be getting the coveted spot in the front from now on too?" Trudy asked her voice laced with sarcasm.

"You're always welcome to leave." Mike touched the brim of his hat and then walked away. He could hear Trudy sputtering behind him, and a smile slid over his face. No matter how many times he brought wagons out to Oregon, it was always the same. There were the gossips, the complainers, the lazy ones, and the ones he wanted to strangle. But those types of people were the exception, and the rest of the folks were good, kind people.

He was glad when the noon break was over and they could continue on.

CHAPTER FIVE

he routine continued the same, day in and day out, over the next two weeks. There was a small group of women that whispered behind their hands whenever she was in sight. The worst part was the way Mike ignored her. She understood, but that didn't make the hurt any less. She looked for him constantly as she drove the wagon. He'd ride by, give her a tip of his hat, and keep going. She thought she had been lonely before, but with this new attitude of his, the feeling had returned in spades. Inside, she wanted to curl up and die. She hadn't realized how much Mike had come to mean to her. She had looked on him as more than a friend and now she was left with pain in her heart.

She had no right to her feelings. After all, she was married to Clancy still. As soon as she found a judge, she was going to have the marriage annulled. But given the fact they hadn't seen anyone in weeks, it wasn't bound to happen anytime soon. Besides, Mike wasn't the type of man to put down roots. He seemed content to travel back and forth across the country.

She'd become very comfortable in the Lewis wagon.

Natalie and her daughter Lily were delightful people. Natalie was still a bit green about some of the chores, but she was willing to learn and that was what counted. Susan got to sleep inside the wagon with them that was an extra bonus. So far, she'd been lucky and had been able to keep out of Clancy's way. She talked to Jed and he found her buck knife that she strapped to the inside of her leg. It wasn't a matter of if it was a matter of when he'd come after her. She often felt his eyes upon her and it always made her shudder.

After a particularly troublesome stretch along the trail, it was time to stop for the day. Even muscles that had grown used to driving the wagon had begun to ache. She slowly climbed down off the wagon and waved to the Motts.

"I heard tell we'll be at the river crossing by tomorrow. Mike asked me to tell you that if one of the men offers to drive your wagon you let them," Savanna said when she came closer. She smiled kindly. "You been doing a good job, and I have to say I feel better knowing you're not with that Clancy. How are the Lewises doing?"

"It's hard, and they're still mourning. But we manage a smile once in awhile. Both Natalie and Lily are very kind hearted. It was good of them to take me in."

"Good. Stop by our fire later for a cup of coffee if you get a chance. I know Clarke would love to talk to you." Savanna waved as she headed back to her wagon.

Susan put her hands on the small of her back and stretched. She had oxen to take care of while Natalie made the fire and put the coffee on. It was a blessing to have somebody helping her. She leaned on Natalie as much as Natalie leaned on her. As she peered around the circle of wagons she spotted Clancy. He was making his own fire in talking to Nellie Walton.

Susan glanced around looking for Nellie's father. He wouldn't be pleased to see his precious daughter with

Clancy. Nellie was a buxom young lady with blond hair and blue eyes. She often had men flocking to her side. Why was she with Clancy?

Clancy and Nellie laughed together and then looked her way. Mortified to have been caught, Susan quickly glanced away. Her face heated as she went about unhitching the oxen. It was disheartening to know she was talked about. Gossip, untruths, and speculation just led to heartache. She'd been through it once, and it had been too much to take. She continued to unyoke and rub down the oxen as memories flooded her mind.

It was just six months ago that she'd been accused of stealing. Her best friend Millie had taken money from her own father. Unbeknownst to Susan, Millie planned to change her name and move. Susan shivered. The people of the town had pointed fingers at Susan. After all, she must have known something. They even went as far as accusing her of being in on the whole mess. Millie's betrayal had torn her apart, and the assumption of others, people she had known since she was born, was the last straw.

Susan had loved Millie's family but in the end it was easier to keep to herself and not be the subject of gossip and false accusations. Not long after that her parents died in an accident with the wagon. There were times when the loneliness was almost unbearable. Now her desperation to go west had placed her as a target for gossip once again.

Pulling her shoulders back she held her head up high as she walked back to the Lewis wagon. She'd done nothing to be ashamed of.

"I've got the coffee and the beans on," Natalie told her with a smile. "It was a great idea to soak them all day. Now I know why mine were inedible."

It was good to see Natalie smile, and Susan couldn't help but smile back. One had to be strong to survive. Lily and

Natalie would be just fine. The three of them would make it to Oregon and start new lives.

Once the food was ready they each placed a wooden crate around the fire and sat.

"Natalie have you given any thought to what you plan to do once you reach Oregon?" Susan regretted asking as Natalie's smile faded.

"There's plenty of time to decide. We're just glad you're here to help us through."

Before she could answer, Mike joined them, towering so much they had to tilt their heads back to see his face. His expression was serious, and the little jolt she'd felt from his presence faded. "Mike, what's wrong?"

He shifted from one foot to the other. "I just wanted to check and make sure you're fine." He smiled and tipped his hat at Natalie and Lily. "Susan, can I talk to you in private?"

She furrowed her brow as she stood. "Of course." She followed him to a spot just beyond the light of the fires. "Mike, what's wrong? You're scaring me."

He turned toward her and even in the dim light she could see the concern he had in his blue eyes. "There's been a lot of talk about you and Clancy, but I'm sure you're aware of that. What you probably don't know is Clancy is trying to get you back. He has made himself sound like the most gracious of husbands, and he can't understand why you left. I don't know how, but a lot of people seemed to side with him, and it's my fear he's going to demand that you travel with him again." Mike reached out and touched her arm.

"He threw me out. I just won't go. There's no reason that demands that I travel with him." She clasped her hands to keep them from shaking. What if Clancy's plan was to trade her for more whiskey?

"I'll do what I can, but if he gets enough people on his side my hand could be forced. I might be in charge but I also need to have the respect and trust of everyone. Those that believe Clancy think that you are a wayward wife with no morals or sense of duty. It's as though they've forgotten how Clancy spent all those days drunk leaving you to fend for yourself."

She stared into his eyes hoping to see an answer, but there wasn't one. "So by keeping my mouth shut and my problems to myself I've done myself a disservice. Is that why women have been flocking over to Clancy's camp every evening? Is he telling some story of woe and gaining sympathy for himself?"

Mike nodded. "I'm afraid so, and I wish I'd known about it sooner so I could put a stop to it. I promised to keep you safe, but he is your husband."

Susan laid her hand over Mike's and gave it a gentle squeeze. "Mike, you've done what you can. It's my mess and I'll deal with it. As long as he's not drinking, things shouldn't be too bad if he demands that I go back to him." She gave him a slight smile hoping that he believed her. He raised his brow and shook his head. "We should go back before they start gossiping about us," she said.

He opened his mouth as though he had something else to say, but nothing came out. He simply walked with her back into the firelight and escorted her to the Lewis wagon.

Susan gave him a smile. "Thanks for warning me. We'll deal with it when the time comes. Have a nice evening." She walked away without turning back and sat at her place next to the fire. Her stomach churned at the thought of being back with Clancy but she kept a smile on her face. She didn't want to burden Natalie or Lily with her problems. She glanced across the circle of wagons and saw Clancy standing staring at her with a smile that promised retribution. Mike couldn't help her, and it wouldn't be fair to put him on the spot. She nodded politely at Clancy and then quickly turned away.

THE NEXT DAY they traveled only six miles before reaching the crossing of the Platte River. Mike was glad to see that there were only a few parties ahead of them.

"Do you think will be able to cross today?" asked Eli.

"Jed should be back at any time to let us know what the timetable is. Meanwhile, why don't we circle the wagons I have a feeling we won't be crossing today. Then I want to call a meeting and explain how to ford this particular river. I don't plan on losing anyone this time." Mike's shoulders were tense with the weight of the responsibility of everyone's lives in his hands.

"I'll have them circle and spread word of the meeting." Eli spurred his horse and was off.

Mike turned Arrow and started a ride in the direction that Jed had gone. He wanted to take a look for himself at the river to see how high it was. The Platte River wasn't usually very high. It was more of a muddy mess that sucked wagon wheels and the oxen's feet down into the river bed. He'd have to remind everyone not to use the river water for drinking unless they let all the silt settle to the bottom. Sometimes bugs had to be skimmed off the top too. It was clean enough for washing and the like. He smiled when he spotted Jed. He slowed Arrow and waited for Jed to catch up to them.

"Just like you said. There's only one decent place to cross. We'll probably go tomorrow afternoon if we're lucky. One of the wagon parties is full of inexperienced drivers. That'll slow things down for sure." Jed smiled. "Looks like we get to rest for a little while."

Mike nodded. "It sure does look like it, little brother." They turned their horses and headed toward camp. The wagons were all circled and the atmosphere felt lighter than it had in days. As long as Clancy didn't stir things up they'd have a fine day.

Smitty already had the big tub filled with a bit of water over the fire. He washed clothes whenever he had a chance. "You two change into some clean clothes and give me those that you're wearing." He didn't wait for an answer or acknowledgment; he always assumed that they'd do what he said and they usually did.

Soon enough Mike, Eli and Jed had washed up and put on clean clothes. Most of the other travelers had done the same. Mike went from wagon to wagon making sure everyone was fine and warned against drinking water from any of the water holes nearby. That water was foul. The whole time he kept his eye on Clancy. He didn't trust him one bit. With his attempts to garner sympathy for himself, no doubt he was up to something, and more than likely it wasn't something good.

The children chased each other through the camp, and most of the people wore smiles on their faces. One man in their group brought out his fiddle and began to play. Soon enough everyone called for a dance after all the evening chores were done. It was nice they were all getting along, but dang, Mike dreaded dances. The single women always wanted to dance with him whether he wanted to or not. Even though it wasn't his favorite thing to do, though, he did enjoy watching Eli, Jed and Smitty out on the dance floor. It amazed him how many husbands refuse to dance with their wives. But he'd have to keep his eyes open to make sure there was no whiskey passed around.

Connie Ranger stood at the back of her wagon and as soon as he approached her he knew it was a mistake. When her father wasn't around, Connie flirted with all the men. A few wives had complained about her, but Mike told them there wasn't a thing he could do about it. He told them to complain to her father, but since Connie's behavior hadn't changed he doubted they had said a word.

"How have you and your father been holding up? Everything all right?" Mike made sure to stand out of her reach.

Her smile widened and her eyes grew sultry. "Hello, Mike. It's so nice of you to come by and check on my welfare. She dropped the ladle she'd been holding, and as she bent to pick it up she made sure he got an eyeful of what was under her dress.

Disgusted he turned away. "I need to check on the rest of the folks."

"Mike, will you be at the dance?"

Mike turned back to her. "I'm assuming most people will be there. Good day." He took long strides to get away from her as quickly as possible.

Next he came across a huddle of women, all whispering. The temptation to groan out loud had to be suppressed. A group of judgmental gossipers wasn't something he wanted to deal with. "Ladies," he greeted as he tipped his hat and hastened to walk past.

"Wait!"

Dang, he'd almost gotten away. He stopped and went back to the group. "What can I do for you?"

Trudy Singleton stepped forward and put her hands on her hips. "For starters, you can get that Susan back into her husband's wagon. It's shameful they live apart. He says he tried everything to make her happy, but she up and left."

"Ladies, it's not my business. Clancy rode in the wagon the first few weeks and didn't help his wife one lick. "You might ask Clancy why he kicked his wife out of their wagon. There are two sides to every story." A few of the women nodded but it was clear the rest didn't agree.

There were a few murmurs. "Honestly, Mike, Clancy was ill. He probably didn't know what he was saying," Trudy insisted. "A wife's place is with her husband. She should be helping him each day, not the Lewises."

"I know you have strong feelings about this, but it's not my call. I hope to see each of you tonight for the festivities." He spotted Eli. "Hey, Eli, wait up." Mike made a beeline for Eli.

Eli frowned. "What's wrong?"

"Nothing. Just some hens squawking. They want me to force Susan to go back to Clancy. Clancy sure has them all fooled. They feel sorry for him."

"That's crazy. Why do you always allow the crazy people to sign on to our party? Every trek west something like this happens. You need to get better at spotting the lunatics." Eli softened his accusation with a grin.

"I usually deal with the husbands when signing people on. Keep an eye out for Susan will you? I don't like where this is all going."

"Sure thing, Mike. Got your dancing boots for tonight?" Eli chuckled as Mike frowned.

"I'll have to find them. They're probably right next to yours."

"I bet they are. Did you want me to talk to the sweet ladies?" Eli asked.

"Nothing more to say, and they aren't so sweet. I need to finish visiting each wagon. I'll see you later." Mike watched Eli walk away. Their parents would have been proud of how responsible both Eli and Jed were. Clancy's wagon was next. He'd might as well get it over with.

"What do you want?" Clancy barked.

"Just checking up on everyone is all."

"You've been checking on my wife an awful lot. Don't think I haven't noticed." Clancy glowered at him.

"I check on everyone, including you. Glad to see you can do for yourself." Mike turned and walked on. He heard

Clancy grumbling but he didn't turn back. No sense in arguing.

He made it back to Smitty. He took off his hat, slapped it against his thigh and then ran his fingers through his hair.

"Hard day?" Smitty asked, sounding amused.

"Same old thing. A bunch of the women aren't happy with Susan living apart from her husband."

Smitty slowly shook his head. "Not exactly the same. You have your eye on that Susan gal."

Mike sighed. "I've been trying to stay away from her. I go out of my way to ignore her, but I'm drawn to her. Knowing her marriage isn't real doesn't help matters."

"Lots of marriages don't start out as *real* but they end up real enough. You'd best stay on the right side of things." Smitty handed him a cup of coffee.

"Thanks. I always try, Smitty, I always try."

WEARY. That was Susan's word for the day. She was weary from the pointed looks, the whispers and laughs apparently about her. How did Clancy manage to convince everyone to be against her? If she hadn't been so busy doing both her work and Clancy's she might have made a few friends. Mostly she kept to herself except for the Lewis and Mott families.

She smiled at Lily as she twirled around in anticipation of the dance. Natalie was still mourning but had agreed to watch for a bit. The Motts both had a sparkle in their eyes, and Susan could tell they couldn't wait for the dancing to begin. If she had her wish, she'd grab some extra sleep, but she'd try to enjoy herself for a little while at least. Maybe she could make a few friends.

As soon as most people had finished their chores the

music started. Mr. McGregor was wonderfully talented with his fiddle. He reminded her of her grandfather with his bushy white hair and long beard. Soon people began to dance.

Susan stood next to Natalie, tapping her foot in time with the music. The gossipy woman kept watching her, but most disturbing was the gleam in Clancy's eye as he stared. A chill ran down her spine. Keeping a smile on her face was hard but she was determined to appear as though she didn't have a care in the world.

She watched as Mike danced with one woman after another. Sometimes his smile looked pained, and Susan wanted to laugh. He was probably getting his feet stepped on. Eli and Jed did their fair share of dancing too. Maybe it was part of the job. No one asked her, which was fine; she was just as content watching.

Clancy smiled at her from across the circle of spectators, and then he began to make his way to her side. "Natalie, I'm going to go back to the wagon."

"Are you feeling poorly?" Natalie asked.

"No, Clancy—"

"May I have this dance?" She'd been so focused on Clancy she hadn't noticed Mike approaching.

She looked at his proffered hand and put hers in it. The warmth rushing through her at his touch made her feel safe. "I'd be delighted."

He led her out to the middle of the crowd and put his arm around her. His touch made her shiver but in a good way. She knew it wasn't the way a married woman should feel with another man, just as she knew if she looked up into his eyes, she'd be lost but she did it anyway. Her breath was momentarily taken away. His gaze, intense and understanding, made her feel as though she was the only woman around for miles.

"You saw Clancy coming my way didn't you?"

"I figured you needed rescuing, but if I'm interfering just say so." He continued to gaze into her eyes.

"No, actually I was just about to leave. I don't want him near me. I do need to talk to him at some point and let him know our sham of a marriage is over. He didn't like me much anyway."

Mike pulled her slightly closer. "He's determined to have you back. There have been murmurs from some of the women about your wifely duties."

Her face heated. "I have no duty to that man. If they don't like me so be it."

Mike didn't answer; he just smiled and continued to dance. Soon the song was over and Mike walked her over to Smitty instead of Natalie. "Thank you for the dance, Susan. Smitty will walk you to your wagon and make sure you don't have any unwanted visitors."

"Thank you." She let go of his hand, and it felt as though she'd let go of a life line. Mike anchored her but without him she was adrift.

Smitty was as wide as he was tall, but his smile gave away the fact that he was more of a gentle giant. "Ready to go, ma'am?" He waited for her nod before he started to walk.

She glanced around, but Mike was nowhere in sight. It was just as well he wasn't the settling down type of man. They reached her wagon, and Smitty bid her a good night before she went inside.

How she wished she could just get divorced. She sighed it wasn't something she could do while they are on their way to Oregon. Imagine those old biddies gossiping about her because of Clancy. She chuckled slightly and shook her head. She had been fooled all right, but a person like Clancy would show his true nature sooner or later.

She must've fallen asleep as soon as her head hit the

pillow. The next thing she knew, it was morning and Natalie and Lily were safe and snug with her. She closed her eyes for a moment, trying to recapture the feeling of Mike's arms around her. Her imagination was nowhere near the real thing.

CHAPTER SIX

*I*t was their turn to ford the Platte River. The morning sun was shining, and they'd all be across well before dark. The Platte River always seemed to take a person from each party that crossed, and Mike prayed that wouldn't be the case today.

He purposely put other wagons ahead of the Mott and Lewis wagon. He didn't want to be accused of favoritism again. So he led the Sugar Tons, the Rangers, and a few of the other complainers across first. He even allowed Clancy to cross over before Susan. Smitty was already on the other side and had a big fire built in case someone fell in and needed to be quickly warmed. They also had men lined along the riverbank for extra safety.

He motioned for Clarke Mott to drive down the bank. The wagons teetered and that always made him nervous. Next came Susan driving the Lewis wagon. Her mouth was shaped into a grim line, and he could tell she had a tight hold on the lines.

"I think I should drive the team," he suggested trying to give her a reassuring smile.

She shook her head. "Everyone else drove their own wagons. I'm sure I can too."

He rubbed the back of his neck recognizing the stubborn look in her eye. "Have a good hold on the traces and follow the path. The poles mark where it is safe for a wagon to travel. Drive slow and steady and don't stop. Just be careful Eli and Smitty are on the other side and they can help you if needed. Good luck." Their gazes met and held, and this time she gave him a smile before she flicked the lines to move the oxen forward.

He really wished she'd let him drive her wagon. He was nervous the whole time waiting and watching and praying. Relief swept through him when the wheels of her wagon were safely up on the other side. He felt like he could breathe easier as he led the other travelers one by one down the bank to the Platte River.

Everyone had crossed, and Mike would've liked for them to all take a rest but they had to keep moving. The two parties ahead of them had already crowded the riverbanks, and he always found nothing but trouble camping near other parties. Whether it was things that were stolen, insults, or the worst sicknesses, something always went wrong. They'd keep going at least

for the next three or four hours.

He hoped everyone had followed his warning about the water around the Platte. He told them to stay away from it but as in all things it was usually one or two who refused to heed his warning. He hoped that wouldn't be the case this time around. Tomorrow they'd come to the North Platte River where the water was plentiful and clean. They'd follow that River for a good long while.

Susan's arms ached from being so tense. The river crossing had been more treacherous than it looked. She should've taken Mike up on his offer and allowed him to drive, but unfortunately, her pride had stood in her way. But they made it, and she was proud of her accomplishments. While helping with supper, she heard some grumbling about people not having enough water.

Why some people didn't listen to Mike and his brothers she didn't know. He had mapped out for them when they should fill the water how much they would need until the next place they would find water. Luckily, she and Natalie worked well together, and they had plenty of water. She wondered if she should offer some but then again it was the same people who had said things about her that seemed to be in dire straits.

Perhaps, if someone came and asked her she'd be happy to share but she wasn't about to offer. Besides, Mike said they'd be near the North Platte River sometime tomorrow. It would be nice to travel along the river for a change. Some days it seemed as though the scenery was the same over and over and over, so anything different was a welcome sight.

"I really admire you," Natalie said. She dished up some stew and handed Susan the plate. Lily was already eating. "You are very brave. It took everything inside me not to scream as we crossed the river."

"Natalie, I felt the exact same way. I'm just grateful that everything worked out fine. You are stronger than you know."

Smitty seemed to appear out of nowhere, and he stopped at the fire. "Susan, Clancy's real sick and is asking for you. Now it's up to you whether you want to come or not, but I'm just thinking how it would look to everyone else if you didn't check on your husband."

Susan felt the blood leave her face, and her heart pounded

faster. She stood up and nodded. "Let me grab some of my things and then we can go."

Natalie stood up to. "Susan, do you want us to come with you?"

Susan crawled up into the wagon, grabbed a few things, and came right back out. "No, absolutely not. If there's a sickness I don't want you or Lily anywhere near it. You just stay put. I don't know how long this is going to take. It could be that I won't return until morning."

Natalie hugged her then stepped back. "If you need anything you send word. You hear me?"

"I will, I promise." Susan hurried away with Smitty at her side. Hopefully, Clancy just broke a finger or something. But as they neared his wagon she knew it was much more serious than that. The first person she spotted was Mike, who turned and gave her a sad smile.

Mike reached out his hand to pull her through the crowd. "He's mighty sick, and it looks like cholera. Now, it's not a death sentence. Some people do pull through, and if there was any other choice, I wouldn't ask you to do this, but he needs you to nurse him. Can I count on you?"

She squeezed his hand. "Of course you can." She held on as Mike helped her up into the wagon, and then she turned away.

The smell inside the wagon was so putrid she wanted to vomit. Clancy lay on the wagon floor holding his stomach and writhing in pain. She'd seen cholera before, and was positive that Clancy had it. Poking her head out of the back of the wagon she yelled to Mike that she needed clean water and for someone to dump out the water in Clancy's barrel.

She rummaged through the wagon to find fresh linens and cloths. She wiped the sweat off Clancy's brow, surprised at the look of hatred on his face.

"It hurts bad, real bad."

"I know, Clancy, I know." She hurried to the back of the wagon when Mike called out that he had the water. She had him pour some into a cup and some into a basin. She then put both near Clancy, wet a cloth and began bathing him.

Cleaning his upper body didn't give her any qualms but she'd have to clean the rest of him, and she'd never seen the rest of them. She shook her head. If she didn't do it, no one else would. She slipped off his soiled clothes and did what she could. Next, she tried to get him to drink some water, but he didn't want any. In fact, he told her to leave but she refused. It only became worse from there.

Clancy's mind wasn't clear, and he didn't seem to know her. He refused to drink, so when he fell into a deep sleep, she took a cloth and dripped water into his mouth. It seemed to work for a while but it just came back up again. He couldn't seem to hold anything down. She felt bad for him he really didn't have anybody. Not one person volunteered to help. She could hear them all outside the wagon whispering to each other. His soiled clothes and bedding lay at the end of the wagon and she quickly threw it all out the back. The resulting screams of disgust made her smile.

An hour later, Mike stuck his head in and said he had some tea Smitty had made for Clancy and a cup of coffee for her.

"Thank you. Are people still standing out there?" She put the cup of tea next to the cup of water and then she held the coffee. It had cooled off enough for her to drink and it tasted wonderful. "Thank Smitty for me too."

"When you threw his contagious clothes out the back of the wagon, everyone scattered. What else can I do for you?"

"There's nothing much to do, but seeing you helps. You know, I really don't know much about Clancy. I know he never married before, he has no children, but that's all I know. I have no idea if he has a mother or father out there if there's anyone to notify in case…"

"You're doing the best you can. Right now, the other things don't matter. The only thing that matters is Clancy's health and yours. I've seen cholera wiped out whole families and a big portion of wagon trains. Make sure you keep your hands clean and wash them after touching him. Don't share a cup or anything else. I want you to stay well." His eyes briefly held his feelings for her, but all too fast it was gone.

"Can you let Natalie know I'll be spending the night here? I don't want her to worry. I've nursed people with cholera before, and I'm being careful. If I can't get him to take water, I don't think I can save him." Her heart felt heavy, and sadness washed over her.

Mike's Adam's apple bobbed up and down as he gazed at her. "Smitty said he'll have some supper out to you. He said he interrupted your meal when he came to get you."

"How long have you known Smitty? He sure is a giant of a man with a great big heart."

"Most my life. My parents died a while back, and Smitty's been helping me raise my brothers. He's been the one constant in our lives. I don't know what we'd do without him."

Clancy cried out in pain, and Susan hurried back to him. She tried to get some tea down him, but he didn't want it. She began dripping the water drop by drop into his mouth. She didn't give him very much at a time, and he kept it down —for the moment, at least. Leaning back against the side of the wagon, she closed her eyes and let the tears roll down her face. Right now, he could go either way, and she hoped he lived. Not that she wanted to live with him again, but she'd never wished him ill.

MIKE SHOOK HIS HEAD, and his eyes grew wide. People never ceased to amaze him. He glanced at Eli and Jed as they sat the morning campfire. Their eyes were wide too. A number of people had come to them asking to leave Clancy and Susan behind. They didn't care that Susan wasn't sick. One of their group even suggested it would be the equivalent of cutting off a toe to save a foot. No one cared that he was going put them at the end of the train and no one offered to help except for the Motts and Natalie. He shook his head. People always started out on the journey as nice, generous people, and somewhere along the way, they turned mean and stingy. All he could hope for was when this crisis was over they turned somewhat nice again.

"I'm going to check on Susan and let her know they'll be at the end of the train today. Jed would you mind driving their wagon?" Mike didn't wait for an answer he marched off into the direction of Clancy's wagon.

The first thing he noticed was a neatly folded pile of the soiled items Susan had thrown out the wagon the previous day. He also saw another pile of extra bedding. Perhaps people weren't as mean as he thought. But the lack of people standing around the wagon was obvious. People just didn't like sickness, and they were afraid. He called out her name softly and waited.

Susan poked out from the back of the wagon. Her long black hair stuck up at odd angles. Blue half-moons lay under her eyes, and the smile she gave him was sad. "It's good to see you, Mike. Clancy is the same, but at least he's no worse. If you could get Smitty to make me more tea for him I'd appreciate it."

"Sure I can do that. Jed's going to be driving your wagon today."

"Perhaps Jed can drive Natalie's wagon, and I can drive this one. I was almost afraid we'd be left behind."

Mike smiled at her. "The Lewis wagon will stay up front where Smitty can keep an eye on Natalie as she drives. She wants to do it, so I thought that we'd give her the chance. Jed's going to drive this wagon. There were a few that wanted you left behind, but you'll be at the end of the train so be prepared for some dust. Smitty is making you a pot of tea, a basket of food and some coffee. I'll have him stop by and grab some of your things from Natalie if that's alright with you."

"Be sure to thank Smitty for me. I'll need some more clean water too if anyone is willing to share. Will we make it to the North Platte River today?"

Mike took off his hat and ran his fingers through his hair. "We should later in the day. I wish there was something I could do to help you. Susan, you look so tired. Did you get any sleep at all?"

"I cat napped here and there," she said, but her cheerful smile seemed forced.

He didn't want her to know just how bad she looked so he nodded. "That's good I'm glad you were able to get some rest. I'll check on you again when we stop for the noon meal." He put his hat back on his head and tipped it toward her. "You take care."

"Mike? Thank you for caring." She pulled her head back into the wagon.

Mike's heart sank. He hoped she didn't end up sick too. He wished he hadn't had to ask her to nurse Clancy, but there'd been no other choice. He turned away from the wagon and was surprised to find plenty of people watching him from a distance.

The Sugar Tons stopped him as he tried to walk by. "We are leaving them behind, aren't we?" asked Trudy Sugarton.

"They'll be riding the tail end of the train. They'll be of no concern to you." He started to walk away when Elton grabbed his arm. Mike looked down at Elton's hand then stared hard into the other man's eyes until Elton unhanded him. "Like I said, they will be of no concern to you." Mike walked away. How he wished he could plant his fist into Elton's face. He heard other people call out to him, but he didn't stop. He didn't have a kind word for anyone at the moment.

Soon enough, everyone was ready, and he yelled, "Wagons ho!" Smitty took the lead, followed by Natalie and the rest of the train with Susan and Clancy in the rear.

It was smooth traveling for them, and they were able to go a bit faster. They covered much more ground than he'd anticipated by the noon meal. They stopped, and he immediately went to see how Susan was. He'd worried about her all morning. What if she caught what Clancy had? What if she died? His heart felt as though it was being clamped in a vise and he was helpless to make it stop.

As he drew closer to the wagon, Jed motioned for him to be quiet. He peeked quietly into the back. Both Clancy and Susan were sleeping. Poor Susan was sitting up with her head at a weird angle. She was bound to have a sore neck when she woke. He eased away and nodded to Jed before he got on Arrow and rode back up to the front of the wagon train. He smiled when he saw the Lewises and the Motts at Smitty's fire. They were good folks.

As soon as he was off Arrow's back, they surrounded him, all talking at once, asking how Susan was faring.

"Right now, she's sleeping and that's a good sign since she looked so tired this morning. I'll have Smitty bring her more tea and food before we leave."

Savanna Mott stepped forward. "Would it be alright if I went down to take a peek?"

Mike shook his head. "I know you're worried about her, but the rest of the travelers are not happy. They expected me to leave both her and Clancy behind and I can't have them getting upset and assuming that the sickness is spreading."

"Hogwash," Savanna said. "I try to be tolerant of others really I do but some people just make me want to scream." The rest nodded in unison.

Mike took the cup of coffee that Smitty offered him. "I think that happens in most communities and that's what we are, a community. We're stuck with each other for months, and I'm trying my best." He took a swig of his coffee and in turn to Natalie. "How'd you do?"

She smiled brightly. "Much better than I ever thought. This whole experience has made me realize just how strong I am. When Susan gets back we can take turns driving."

"Good, that's good to hear. We should be near the North Platte River by the end of the day. I'll have Jed watch Clancy while you ladies take Susan for a much-deserved dip in the river."

Lily clapped her hands together. "Yea, for going swimming."

Mike smiled. It was nice to make at least one person happy.

His smile of making it to the North Platte River faded when they stopped for the night. He motioned for them to circle the wagons, watching as each driver pulled the wagon into the right position, but before the last wagon was part of the circle men had gathered and blocked Jed from joining. Dang, the possibility of death scared people stupid. He urged Arrow to move forward.

"What's going on here?" He recognized many men he'd thought to be reasonable.

Ranger stepped forward, rifle in hand. "We're not allowing that sick, diseased wagon in with ours. You might be sweet on Susan, but that doesn't mean you can put our lives in danger."

Much of the crowd yelled in agreement.

Mike stared at Jed, who had a rifle across his lap. These men meant business, and he couldn't put his brother in harm's way. He raised his hand to quiet the unruly crowd. "Listen, you know I wouldn't have had Jed drive the wagon if I thought cholera was contagious. You have to be careful is all. But, if you all feel so strongly about this, I'll have Jed drive the wagon outside of the circle and next to mine."

"We want them to just turn around and go in another direction!" someone shouted.

Mike sighed. "That's the best I can do. By rights, I have the authority to allow them inside the camp, but I'm listening to what you have to say, and I'm making a reasonable compromise." He stared at each man until they nodded and looked away. All except for Ranger.

"We'll go along with it for now but this isn't the end of it!" Ranger shouldered his way through the crowd and headed to his wagon.

Mike nodded to Jed who drove away and around the wagons. Jed stopped the wagon next to Smitty's, close but not too close. Jed was smart.

Susan peeked out the back of the stopped wagon. How could people be so cruel? A shudder rippled through her, and she wrapped her arms around her waist. They'd have their wish soon enough. Clancy was getting worse, and she couldn't get him to keep anything down. The wagon was filled with soiled clothes, and this time she didn't dare throw them outside. She didn't need to be lynched or banned.

She stretched to get rid of some of the tension building inside of her. She needed to get out of the wagon but she couldn't, not with the other people being so hostile. It was good to see Smitty motioning for her to come out, though. When he offered his hand, she took it and was glad of his assistance in getting her down. "Thank you."

"I'm not sure if you heard what went on, but you need to stay with the wagon," he told her.

"I heard every word. I'll abide by the rules. Is that a river I hear?" She asked.

"Straight through those bushes but don't go near it for now. Most of the folks are headed there to bathe and the like. How's Clancy?"

Despair choked her, making speaking difficult. "Worse, and I fear he may die."

Smitty nodded and grabbed a crate from the wagon. "Here, sit in the fresh air for a bit. I don't think anyone will bother you."

"You've been so kind to us, Smitty. I appreciate it." She tried to summon a smile but it wasn't possible.

Smitty's face turned bright red. "You just sit for a spell, and I'll have some food for you soon."

It felt nice to sit in the open air. She waited for Smitty to leave before she allowed tears to fall. Seeing Jed come back from tending the oxen, she hurriedly wiped her tears away. He didn't need to see her cry.

"It'll be just fine, Susan," he said. "How's Clancy?"

"Not good. We'll probably know by morning if he'll live. It makes me so mad. Why didn't he listen? Why did he drink that awful, foul water? It makes no sense."

Jed nodded. "I wish I had an answer for you."

"Go, get some coffee and relax. You put in a full day driving." She couldn't keep her voice from breaking.

"I should stay."

"No, please, Jed. I'd like to be alone for a bit if you don't mind."

He hesitated as he gazed at her and nodded. "I'll be back to check on you."

Tears threatened again, so she just nodded, and as soon as he was out of sight she had a good cry. But she only allowed herself to cry for a few minutes. She had too much to do. Now that there was plenty of water she needed to bathe Clancy again, wash his bedding and bathe herself.

She poured a good amount of water into the basin, set it in the wagon, and then carefully got back in. Clancy had his faults but he didn't deserve to die like this. Bathing him might be futile but it was the least she could do for him. His body had changed in just a day. He looked bluish and so sunk in. It was almost as if he'd shriveled.

He was out of it and didn't recognize her. He called for his mother, and Susan answered him. It seemed to bring him a sense of peace. She was able to put the last of the clean bedding under him. It wouldn't be long before those, too, became soiled.

After gathering all that needed to be washed, she jumped down from the wagon and made a fire. She'd need hot water to clean his things. She dragged the washtub out of the wagon and began to heat the rest of her water. It would have to do until she could go and get more. Someone had changed out the water barrel with a clean, filled one.

It was a good bet it was either the Todd brothers or Smitty. They'd all been so kind to her. They made her feel worthy again. It was a part of her that had been stripped from her by her family and the people of her town. Even through tragedy she was healing.

After she poured hot water into the tub, she let the clothes soak for a bit. It was going to take a lot of lye soap to get any of it clean again. It wasn't an easy job, the hot water burned her hands and the lye soap stung leaving her hands raw, but she got it done. She hung the wet things on the tree branches and bushes around her.

The sounds of laughter and happy cries drifted from the river, and Susan knew the women and children were taking a turn bathing. She'd ask someone to refill her water, and then she'd be able to get clean. Next, she checked on Clancy again. Her gut clenched at his harsh and labored breathing. The end was nearing. She'd known deep down he'd die, but she'd hoped and hoped.

As promised, Smitty came by with food and coffee. He didn't have time to stay, but the Motts came and sat with her around her fire. They did their best to be cheery, but Susan was so tired she couldn't keep her eyes open.

"I'm so very grateful for the way you have both stood by me. You have from the very beginning, and it means so much to me." Susan took a deep breath and willed her eyes to remain tearless. There would be plenty of time to cry later.

"You've become very dear to us." Savanna stood and gave Susan's hand a quick squeeze. "We'll check on you in the morning."

Clarke nodded. "You get some rest."

She nodded as she watched them walk back into the wagon circle, leaving her with only the lazy chirp of crickets. The sun was setting, and it would soon be dark. She watched as pink and purple hues took over the sky until the sun was gone. She finished eating and tidied up the campsite. It was time to go and check on Clancy.

She sat down next to him and wiped his brow. His face contorted in pain, and then he breathed his last breath. Her shoulders sagged as he lay ever so still. Before she had a chance to weep she felt the wagon move from side to side. Turning around she saw Mike climb in.

He took one look at Clancy and gave her a sad smile.

"Grab some things. I'm taking you to the river. I'll be right back." He climbed back out.

Numbly she placed a cloth over Clancy's face, and then she grabbed soap, a towel, her nightgown, and a wrap. People would think her scandalous bringing her nightgown but she was beyond caring. She took her things and waited outside the wagon. It was warm out, but her body felt chilled to the bone. What about Mike's rule of no single females? It probably didn't apply to her, now that she was a widow.

A widow. The words echoed in her mind. How did she ever get to be here? One's life could change at any moment. If there was any lesson to be learned from the last few months it was that. Hold dear to what you have. You could lose it all in a heartbeat.

Mike walked into the firelight and held out his hand. She grasped it as a lifeline and let him lead her to the river. As attentive as he was, he'd make a woman a good husband someday if he ever settled down. She could feel his strength in his touch.

He stopped by the river and peered into her face. "You seem troubled. I wish there was something I could do to take your pain away."

The moon wasn't full, but it gave off enough light to see his earnest expression. She felt so full of doubt. What would her future hold? "Thank you for caring."

"Of course. We're friends. I wouldn't leave you to the mercy of the camp's naysayers. You haven't done anything wrong, and you don't deserve anything but kindness and the highest regard. Now I'll turn my back and you take a swim."

He turned his back before she had a chance to nod her head. Tears flowed, and she didn't even try to stop them. She undressed, grabbed her soap, and walked into the river. It was cool, she supposed but it didn't feel cold to her chilled body. It felt so good to wash herself. She even sighed as she washed her hair. Tears continued to roll down her cheeks and drip into the water below. She'd lost so many people of late. It didn't seem fair.

She wished she could stay in the water, but she made it short. Mike was taking time out of his night to help her. She wouldn't keep him any longer than necessary. She emerged from the river, quickly dried herself off, and put her night-gown on. Then she pulled her wrap around her and grabbed her things.

"I'm done. Thank you so much. It felt wonderful." She tried to smile at him when he turned, but the concern in his blue eyes was too much. She began to weep again.

Mike reached down and lifted her up. He then sat down on a felled log with her on his lap and held her while she cried. His strong arms around her gave her the strength to stop crying. She laid her head on his broad shoulders and breathed in his scent. He smelled like leather and soap. She gave herself one more final moment to make a memory of the embrace. Feeling safe and liked was something she wanted to hold on to.

"We should go, Mike. Thank you for everything." She stood and straightened her gown. She waited for him to stand before she started back. Without his arms around her, the world seemed daunting.

She was surprised to see so much activity at her wagon. Clancy had been wrapped and removed. A grave was dug not too far away. Natalie was on her hands and knees washing the wagon floor. The sides of the canvas were pulled up to air the wagon out. She wasn't without friends. From the look of it, she had all she needed. Wearing her nightgown made her feel strange as though she'd been doing something she hadn't.

Savanna led her to her stool by the fire and handed her a cup of tea. "Warm yourself."

"But I should be the one to clean the wagon."

"You've done so much already, my dear," Savanna said. "Let us help you. We wanted to help with Clancy, but it wasn't allowed. We would have been asked to leave the train. So here we are. You relax."

Susan looked for Mike but there was no sight of him. She watched as Jed, Eli and Smitty laid Clancy in the ground. "They'll say some words tomorrow," Savanna said. "With it being cholera and all…"

Numbly she nodded and stared at his body as it was covered with dirt.

"Burn the wagon!"

She snapped out of her musings and looked to see who was talking. It was Elton Sugarton. *It figures. Do they live to stir up trouble?* She stood and put her hands on her hips. "They'll be no burning of my wagon."

"Your wagon? I thought you left your husband." Elton sneered.

Trudy stepped forward. "He told us all about you and how you refused to do your wifely duty. You should be ashamed of yourself. He suffered because of you!"

Susan's face burned. "How dare you speak about private affairs. It is none of your business. Now please leave."

Trudy laughed. "Not so private. He told anyone who would listen. If the wagon belongs to anyone it belongs to Nellie Walton. She spent plenty of time with Clancy."

"I see," Susan said, but she didn't see, she didn't understand.

"Nellie could be carrying his babe for all we know!" Trudy shouted.

Feeling faint, Susan sat back down. Her shoulders slouched under all the weight that had just been heaped upon them, but she immediately sat up straight and hoped she looked like the queen of England when she lifted her chin. "I don't care what you think you may know or what Clancy may have said. It's not your business anymore."

Elton took a step forward. "The wagon still burns. It contains sickness!"

Natalie jumped down out of the wagon, wiped her hair out of her face and glared at Elton. "You are a fool Mr. Sugarton! Clancy was sick from the water he drank. He was told not to but he did anyway. I'm almost done scrubbing the wagon down, and if I believed there was any type of sickness, believe me, I wouldn't be here. I have a daughter to think about. So, unless you have intentions of helping Susan, I'd suggest you go back to your own wagon."

Everyone was quiet. Natalie was more of a mild-mannered type of person, and it was so out of character for her to yell that everyone seemed stunned.

Bart Bigalow held his hand up. "I'll buy the wagon from Mrs. Willis. How 'bout it, Susan? You'll get money and we can burn the wagon before we leave tomorrow."

Susan sized up big, bad, Bart Bigalow. There was something in it for him, though she couldn't see how. "Thank you for the offer, but the wagon belongs to me, and it will stay mine as I drive it to Oregon." She stared daggers at Bart. But her stare wasn't enough to wilt his evil grin.

She felt warmth behind her and immediately knew it was Mike. Her heart stopped beating in fear. The crowd was starting to turn ugly. Taking a deep breath she began to calm.

———

MIKE SQUELCHED the urge to punch a few people in the face. Troublemakers, every one of them. He stared at each person until they looked away even Nellie Walton. He'd heard most of what had been said as he'd walked to the wagon. If Nellie was indeed carrying, it was her father's problem. She had no claim here.

"Time to call it a night folks. Go on back to your wagons. If you want to pay your respects we'll say a few words over Clancy's grave tomorrow. Good night." His tone of voice invited no answer. It was a blessing to see them all turn and leave. He really didn't want to get into a fight but he wouldn't shy away either.

He turned to Susan. Her eyes were filled with admiration, and he felt ten feet tall. He gave her what he hoped was a reassuring smile. "Don't you worry. It'll all work out. I'll get you to Oregon, and you can start a new life." He wanted to take his words back. He wanted to take her into his arms, hold her, and never let her go. She filled his heart, and he had a feeling he'd end up with a big, ole heartache. Every time he gazed upon her he was a goner. It wasn't just because she was beautiful or that she smiled back at him. It was because of her inner light that shone through in everything she did. She seemed to brighten the whole world when she was around. He'd tried to puzzle out what it was exactly, but it wasn't just one thing. There was something special to everything about her.

"Are you alright? They were becoming a bit demanding."

"A bit?" She turned and nodded toward all of her friends. "I have the greatest friends on earth. I wasn't frightened because of them. I'm more outraged that those people think they can tell me what to do. What did they mean about Nellie? I saw her at the wagon talking to Clancy a few times but…"

"It doesn't matter," Mike said "Why don't you sleep with Natalie and Lily tonight?"

"No, I'm not leaving the wagon. They might burn it."

She had guts. "Fine, I'll sleep under it and make sure you're safe," he told her.

"I'm not sure that's a good idea," she whispered as she blushed.

"It'll be fine. We're friends and I don't want anything to happen to you. You won't even know I'm there."

Later, as he lay beneath her wagon his words came back to haunt him. He wished he didn't know she was there, mere feet from him. He heard her sniffle, and knew she was crying. She'd been through the wringer taking care of Clancy and facing down the crowd. He groaned as he turned over. All he wanted to do was hop in the wagon and hold her. But who was he fooling? Holding her would never be enough.

He rolled over again and sighed. He'd have to find some way to forget her. He couldn't think of her in that way. He wasn't ready to get married. He still had Eli and Jed to take care of. The three of them needed to stick together no matter what, and marrying would mean staying in Oregon. He shuddered.

They'd always planned to settle down on their land but not anytime soon. They'd finished building their house two years ago, and they had some cattle but they always ended up heading back east to guide more people to Oregon. The money was good, and it was something they did well together. Maybe in a few years. What would Susan be doing in a few years? Would she be married with children? It was just as well he'd be away as it would be hard to see Susan with a man she loved. Very hard.

From the sound of it, she wasn't getting much sleep in the wagon. She tossed and turned almost as much as he. Even though she didn't love Clancy, she probably mourned his passing. She was a widow now. Hopefully, she wouldn't draw all the unmarried men to her. It wasn't something she did on purpose. But he'd seen the look in many a man's eye when they gazed at her.

He heard the changing of the guards and decided to get

up. There was no sense in thinking about what couldn't be anymore, and he wasn't one to feel sorry for himself. He and his brothers always dusted themselves off and kept going. Their father had been like that too. He started to roll out when he saw big feet at the end of the wagon.

Quicker than a rattler could strike, Mike was out of his spot. He raised his gun. "Hold it right there!"

Big Bart looked in Mike's direction and took a step back. He raised his hands in the air. "I was just checkin' on the widow. I was hoping she'd changed her mind about sellin' the wagon."

"Do you usually conduct business in the wee hours of the morning?" Mike heard a rifle being cocked and he knew Smitty stood behind him.

Big Bart dropped his hands. "I couldn't sleep. I figured if she'd sell I could get her stuff put into the Lewis wagon for her. I was just trying to be helpful is all." His stare was long and steady.

"It's best you leave. Mrs. Willis needs her sleep. She already told you she isn't selling. I don't want you bothering her about it again."

Bart spit on the ground. "She could still change her mind. I'll mosey on. No harm done." Bart walked back the way he came leaving Mike with a feeling of unease.

"You'd best keep your eye on that one," Smitty said.

"Yeah, I know. I'm going to get Susan's fire going. I won't be able to sleep."

"Have at it, Mike. She's going to need her friends in the coming days." Smitty made his way back to the wagon circle.

"He frightens me," Susan whispered to him from the back of the wagon.

"Well, he's not the most likable fella. Try to get some sleep; it's going to be a long day. I'll have Jed drive your wagon."

She poked her head out. "You most certainly will not. I'm able to drive my own wagon, thank you very much."

"But—"

"Mike, listen. Folks already think you do me too many favors. I don't want them coming after me with pitchforks. I know that you'll be watching out for me. I'll be just fine." She withdrew back behind the canvas.

Mike sighed. She was probably right but he couldn't help but worry.

CHAPTER SEVEN

*T*he days spent traveling along the Platte River were good days. There was plenty of water, plenty of fresh meat, and they even had fish. People were too busy washing clothes and enjoying their bounty to bother with her. It was a nice reprieve. Very nice indeed. Susan tied her bonnet on and was ready for the signal to start the day.

Even though people had left her alone, she always felt as though someone was watching her, and when she peered around she'd usually spot Big Bart staring. It was a bit disconcerting, and she tried to follow Savanna's advice and ignore it but that wasn't so easy. Had Clancy traded her to that man? It wasn't too hard to imagine he had, but she would never go along with it. It was a shame how low whiskey had brought Clancy down. It had made him crazy enough to drink tainted water.

She shook her head. There was no sense going over and over Clancy's death. She'd just finished organizing the wagon when Mike yelled for them to start and off they went. No one was causing trouble while they were on the trail. No one had idle hands. Well, except for the gossipy women.

A strong gust of wind alerted her to the sky. She stared in horror at the angry dark bluish gray colored clouds. The wind kicked up something fierce. It was going to rain and she hadn't thought to put Clancy's duster near the front within her reach. She'd be drenched for sure. Many of the walkers jumped up into their wagons for shelter.

The skies opened, and an amazing amount of rain burst from the clouds. A gully washer for sure. Gusts of wind slanted the deluge sideways, and it was hard to see far ahead through the downpour. She could make out the wagon ahead of her, though, and as long as she could see it she'd be fine. She tried to remember where she'd seen Clancy's coat, and if she was correct, she just might be able to grab it and still drive.

With a firm grip on the lines she turned to one side and reached around. No coat. She turned the other way and almost drove off the trail. Sitting back down, she felt lucky to still be following the wagon ahead of her. So intent on keeping in line, she was startled when Mike rode up next to her. She was even more startled when he jumped off Arrow and onto her wagon.

"I'll drive for a bit. Go in and get something dry on."

The wind almost carried his words away but she was able to hear him. Nodding, she gave him the lines. Then she held onto him as she climbed into the wagon. A shiver wracked her body. The temperature was plummeting. Quickly, she changed into warmer, dry clothes. She found Clancy's coat and his hat and put them on then carefully climbed back out.

"I'm fine now! Thank you!" she yelled above the wind.

Mike nodded. "We'll stop in a bit. I want us a ways from the river in case it floods. I saw you almost turn off back there. Are you alright?"

"Yes, I was trying to find this coat. I realized my folly just in time. Go! Help another damsel in distress. I'm fine, really."

He gazed at her long and hard before he handed the lines back to her. He whistled and Arrow was back beside the wagon. Mike reached out and grabbed the horn of his saddle and the next thing she knew he was riding away. He'd warmed her inside and out. He'd been distant after the night Clancy died. She knew he wasn't interested in her, but she'd thought they were friends. Now, he routinely sent one of his brothers or Smitty to check on her. When he'd talked to her, she had felt a bit less alone in the world. When he'd drawn back, she felt more alone than ever. Her shoulders sagged as dejection threatened to overwhelm her. She wished they could just sit and talk but he didn't seem to want that.

Lightning snapped across the sky, and the hair on the back of her neck stood up. She couldn't see the river, but that didn't mean much. It was hard to see anything. Thunder boomed, and it was getting harder and harder to hold the oxen on course. Her arms were on fire, but she willed herself to keep going. She wondered how Natalie was doing; she could only hope she and Lily were dry. Just as her arms lost all feeling except the burn of protesting muscles, the wagon in front of her turned, and she followed it, taking her place in the circle. Jed came by and alerted everyone to the fact that the livestock needed to be brought inside the circle to keep them from running off.

Susan wished she could just crawl into the back of the wagon but she needed to take care of the oxen. Out into the downpour she went, keeping her head bent to avoid getting blinded by the rain. Puddles had already begun to form, and the wind whipped fiercer than ever.

"Come stay in our wagon!" Clarke yelled.

She shook her head. "I'll be just fine. Thank you, though," she shouted.

He gave her a quick nod and was soon out of sight. Quickly, she let the oxen loose and then climbed into the

KATHLEEN BALL

wagon. After taking Clancy's coat off she wrapped herself in a blanket. The wind rocked the wagon back and forth.

What if it toppled over? Drawing her knees up to her chest, she laid her head on them. The thunder, lightning, and wind were all conspiring to fray her nerves. Maybe she should have taken Clarke up on his offer. A huge banging against the back end of her wagon made her jump. Puzzled, she crawled to the back and peered out.

Big Bart had one hand on her wagon and the other holding his hat on.

"What are you doing here?" she asked, more annoyed than afraid.

"Just checking on my wagon." He gave her an eerie grin.

"It's my wagon, and I want you to stay away from it and me." She hoped she sounded braver than she felt.

"You only think it belongs to you. Clancy lost it in a card game. I won both the wagon and you." He reached inside.

She screamed and grabbed her buck knife. She'd never attacked another human but she didn't have a choice. She lifted the knife and stabbed Bart's hand with all her strength. His resulting bellow gave her pause, but she lifted the knife again waiting for Bart's hand to reappear. When it didn't she scanned the area behind her wagon, but it was too hard to see through the rain.

Her heart beat painfully against her ribs, and a lump formed in her throat. Could it be true? Did Clancy bet the wagon and her? She was more afraid the wagon might not truly belong to her than she was of Bart winning her. Bart might have a case for taking her wagon away, but he had no right to her.

"Oh Clancy, how could you have seemed so compassionate and caring when you were really a scoundrel of the worst sort?" Her words were carried away by the wind. Frightened, she scrambled and grabbed the musket. Her

84

father had taught her how to use one. She put out the oil lamp so she didn't cast any shadows and then sat in the middle of the wagon. Big Bart wouldn't stay gone for long.

As tempted as she was to run to the Mott wagon, she couldn't bring trouble down on them. So she sat in the dark and waited. Every noise startled her, and it was a loud night. The rain kept falling steadily. Her back was sore, and sleeping would have been nice, but she refused to take the risk.

Her intuition paid off. A few hours later, Bart's hand appeared and she stabbed him again. How stupid could he be? She'd thought for sure he'd try to come in the front of the wagon. She smiled as he yelped in pain. Lifting the musket, she aimed for the back and waited once again. It wasn't a heavy gun, but it seemed heavy after holding it up for so long.

The sound of ripping canvas caught her attention and she turned around. He was cutting through it with his big knife. She didn't have time to think she pushed the barrel out the hole he'd made and shot. Next she took her knife and was ready for him to come at her, but Bart started screaming in pain. She inched to the hole and looked out. Bart was holding the side of his head.

"She shot my ear off!" he yelled to someone. She couldn't see who.

Susan sat back in the middle of her wagon as she reloaded the musket. Her body shook, and fear clutched her heart. The constant thunder made it impossible to hear what was going on. A flash of lightening illuminated a man outside her wagon, and she picked up the musket and aimed.

"Susan! Are you alright?"

She let out a breath she didn't even realize she was holding. "Yes. Yes!" she called out to Mike.

He popped his head in the wagon and took his time

looking her over as though he was looking for injuries. "I'm coming in, put the rifle down."

She glanced from him to the musket, and her eyes widened. "I shot him." The words echoed inside her head, and she gripped the gun tighter. She couldn't seem to let it go. It was a relief when Mike crawled in and took it from her. "I stabbed him too. Oh, my."

"I'm sorry you had to go through that, but you did what was necessary to defend yourself. Bart was mumbling something about owning both your wagon and you when Smitty took him to get bandaged up." He sat behind her and pulled her between his legs until her back was against his chest.

When he wrapped his strong arms around her she felt so safe and valued as she never had in her life. She leaned back into him and drew from his strength. They were silent for a bit and she enjoyed being in his arms.

"Is there anything in this wagon Bart would want?" he asked.

"I don't think so. He told me that Clancy lost both the wagon and me in a card game." Her voice cracked.

"I don't condone gambling in my party. Don't worry about any debts of Clancy's from gambling. They won't count, and I'll make sure Bart knows that. We should make it to Fort Laramie in a few days. It's going to be a hard go with all the mud, but it's nothing we haven't done before. I have a feeling we'll have repairs to make on wagons in the morning. Many canvases have holes in them. We'll inspect the wagons before we head out. There are a few wagons that aren't being taken care of. The wheels aren't being greased properly. Best to take care of it before we try to get through the mud.

"You'd best check mine. I didn't know about greasing the wheels."

"Yours and Natalie's have been taken care of on a regular basis."

"I never saw—"

"Eli did it. He hates to be thanked all the time, so he does plenty people don't know about. It's just his way."

"You're so good with them. I see why they look up to you."

He tightened his arms around her and gave her a squeeze. "We've had a few rough years, but they are both young men to be proud of. Someday we'll settle on our ranch. I'm not sure when. Guiding people west suits us for now."

Would he ever truly settle down? Somehow, she couldn't picture it. She tried to tell herself it didn't matter, but deep down, a tiny voice whispered that it did. She had feelings for him. Feelings she tried to deny, but it was no use. They were there, and she had to try to squash them. There was most likely a damsel in distress on every train.

"Try to get some sleep. It'll be a long day tomorrow." He hesitated before he pulled his arms away."

Disappointment flowed through her. "Of course. Thank you for coming to my rescue." She pulled away from him.

Mike smiled. "It looked as though you had everything handled." He laughed.

"It's not funny! I could have killed him."

"You'd have been within your rights. He tried to attack you. He'll be put on notice that he only has one more chance before we ban him."

The blood drained from her face. "Ban him? I'd best watch my back."

Mike nodded. "You need to be vigilant, but me and the boys will keep an eye on you."

Susan nodded. "Thank you."

Mike climbed out of the wagon then looked back at her. "Get some sleep." He was gone before she could respond.

THE STORM LEFT AS QUICKLY as it came. Mike drank his coffee as he watched the sun come up. He sighed; the ground was full of puddles and deep mud. It would be hard going today, but they'd get through it. A positive attitude gave the rest of the party hope. Word of Bart's visit to Susan's wagon had tongues wagging early. Some of the women went from fire to fire to talk and then after they ate they formed a small grouping. He didn't need to hear them to know they somehow blamed Susan. He stood and made his way through the mud to Susan's wagon. She hadn't made a fire but she sat outside of her wagon, holding her head high.

"Did you eat?"

She nodded. "The Motts made enough for me and the Lewises. Clarke sure has a way with fire making. I swear he could make a fire in any conditions. They even invited me to place my coffee pot on their fire. Would you like some?"

The hopeful expression on her face twisted his gut. "I wish I could, but people are talking enough as it is. Has anyone said anything to you?"

A look of sadness enveloped her. "No, they always think they know the truth of every matter. I try to be a nice person, and I can't for the life of me figure out what I ever did to get on their bad side."

"Susan you are the sweetest, nicest woman I know. You'll probably never know why and there probably isn't a valid reason. They just like to gossip, and I'm sorry as can be that they picked you to gossip about." He glanced over his shoulder at the women and nodded at them. "I know it's hurtful, but you didn't bring this upon yourself. It's going to be rough going today with all the mud. Remember, don't stop unless you have to. Go around a stopped wagon if possible."

She smiled at him and his heart warmed. "I'll do my best."

"I know you will. If anything comes up—and I mean anything—just let one of us know. I'll check on you later."

"Thanks for stopping by."

He tipped his hat to her and then walked on to the next wagon. Her blue eyes drew him in and he never tired of gazing at her. Her sweetness and generosity of heart shined through in everything she did. He wished... He wasn't a man for wishes.

He approached the group there was no help for it. "Ladies. It'll be hard walking today but we need the wagons as light as possible."

"Of course, Mike," Connie Ranger said as she smiled at him. "What are we going to do about the Susan problem?"

"Excuse me?" He frowned. "Susan is not nor has she ever been a problem."

"Tell that to Bart," Trudy Sugarton quipped.

"Bart tried to get into her wagon last night, and she defended herself. I would think you'd have more concern for the women on this wagon train. Especially a woman alone." Most of the women looked away but not Connie or Trudy. "How would you have felt if someone tried to come into your wagon? He even tried to slice through the canvas to get to her. No one should be subjected to such a thing. Now I suggest you ladies go back to your wagons and get ready to leave." He couldn't help the anger in his voice. Why did people act this way? He continued on from wagon to wagon, making sure all was ready. Jed and Eli had also made the rounds making sure all the wagon wheels were in good shape. It was time.

"Captain Todd!" A woman raced toward him. He recognized her as Mrs. Wicker. She was always meticulously dressed but today she was sodden and her hair looked to be a tangled mess.

"Ms. Wicker, what's wrong?"

"It's my girl Livie. She went to get water and fell in. The current took her away! Please help us!"

"Jed, Eli ride down river and see if you can spot her! I'll start where she went in and look." All three quickly mounted up and raced along the river bank. Mike stopped at the place where Livie had gone in. He scanned the area and his heart skipped a beat when he saw blood on the hanging tree branch. It did not bode well for the girl.

His head whipped around in the direction of Jed's yell. Mike turned Arrow and raced down the river bank. Jed held Livie in his arms and by the way she lay, Mike knew she was dead. The poor girl couldn't have been any older than ten years old.

All three brothers rode back to camp with Livie cradled on Jed's lap. Mr. Wick stepped forward and took his child into his arms. Unshed tears clouded his eyes. "Thank you for finding my gal. We'll take time to bury her before we go?"

"Of course we will." Mike slide off Arrow and gathered a few men to dig a grave. It was heart wrenching to watch as Livie Wick was buried. They had no choice, they had to move on. There were many tears but unfortunately death was a big part of going west.

"Wagons ho!" he yelled halfheartedly a while later. The men pushed each wagon, one by one, out of the ruts they were in, and they all slowly got going. He hadn't bothered to stop at Bart's wagon. He'd been fighting the urge to hit the man. Although his head was bandaged, Bart drove his own wagon. How he did so with cut hands and his ear nearly blown off, he didn't know.

They were able to travel further than he'd thought. If their luck held out they'd make it to Fort Laramie end of day tomorrow.

"Mike, hold up!" Eli yelled as he rode his horse alongside Mike's. "Bart really has it stuck in his craw the Willis wagon is his. I asked if he had a bill of sale, since gambling wasn't allowed. I even asked if anyone else was a witness to the transaction, but no on both accounts. I told him that the matter was now closed."

Mike nodded. "You did well. I'm proud of you. You'll be leading your own party one day." Mike smiled but the thought of Eli on his own wasn't something he wanted to contemplate. They'd always been a team, him, Eli, and Jed, and of course Smitty. His brothers were becoming grown men. Pride and sadness filled him. Pride for how well they could handle themselves and sadness that someday they'd want families of their own. Heck, he was turning into an old mother hen.

That night Mike wandered over to Bart's wagon to have a chat. Bart threw quite the glare at him. "I wanted to see how you're holding up. I can find someone to drive your wagon if necessary."

Bart spit on the ground. "I ain't asking for any favors from you."

"I know. I was just concerned. I'm confused by a few things. You say that you won both the wagon and Susan? How can that be when gambling is forbidden along the trail?"

"It ain't your business. That wagon is mine, and so is that hellcat. It was all fair and square. No gambling took place. He wanted whiskey, but had no money. He traded me the wagon and his wife for it. I was to take possession of both at the end of the trail. I'm opening a saloon and I'll need a few girls to tend to the men. I'll keep my distance for now, but once we're in Oregon you'll have no say. None at all." He gave Mike a snide grin.

Mike narrowed his eyes. "Now, which is it? Did you win her or did you trade for her?"

"It's the same outcome either way. Since gambling isn't

allowed I'd have to say Ole Clancy traded." Bart smiled even wider.

"I don't have time for your games. As long as you leave her be while she's in my care that's all I can ask." Mike walked away. Bart would leave Susan alone for a while. It gave them time to figure out how to keep her safe in Oregon. Perhaps she could find another husband. His stomach clenched. Was nothing easy?

All he really wanted to do was go to Susan, lift her into his arms, and kiss her breathless. That wasn't going to happen.

THE NEXT MORNING Susan was excited. They'd be at Fort Laramie hopefully by nightfall. It was something new to think about instead of Clancy and Bart and little Livie's death. When was the last time she'd been carefree? In a lot of ways she felt older than her years. Life certainly had its twists and turns, and she was trying her best to bend with them. Hopefully, she'd be able to do some trading. Clancy had left her penniless. But she had enough food to make it through. That was the important thing. It felt as though it had been forever since she'd seen buildings, and there was an overall sense of anticipation in the camp.

Some of her excitement waned as she passed what seemed to be one grave after another. There seemed to be so many, too many. Unease eventually replaced any eagerness she had to go on to Fort Laramie. She clutched her musket close as they drove near a group of Indians who were traveling in the same direction. A shiver went up her spine. Were they the fierce Sioux Indians she'd been told she'd see? They didn't seem to be hostile. In fact they seemed more curious about the wagon party. They were scantily dressed making her feel uncomfortable so she avoided staring at them.

She expected to hear Mike call for them to circle the wagons but they continued on, both parties passing each other. They were surprisingly peaceful, not at all the way they'd been described in the guide books. When she spotted the Fort up ahead the tension in her arms and shoulders began to ebb. She felt more exposed more vulnerable traveling without a husband. Did Natalie feel the same?

A few other wagon trains had arrived at Fort Laramie ahead of them, and she couldn't help but wonder if the graves they passed belonged to the other parties. Once stopped, she took care of the oxen and headed toward the Motts'. Natalie and Lily were already there along with a nice man named Wilber Tone. A handsome man, he was traveling to Oregon with his brother. He seemed to have taken a liking to Natalie and Lily.

"I'm glad to see we're all fine. I have to admit I was frightened when we passed the Indians," she said as she joined them.

"I was too," Natalie admitted.

"I wouldn't have let anything happen to you or Lily," Wilber said, and then he blushed. Natalie blushed too, and Susan was happy for her friend.

"Carter and Wilber are going to escort us to the store. You'll join us, won't you?" Savanna asked.

"I'd love to! Let me grab a few items I'm hoping to trade." Without waiting for an answer she hurried to her wagon and grabbed some of Clancy's clothes. Then she rejoined the group.

"Let's go," Carter said as he held out his arm for Savanna to take.

They took the ferry across the river, walked up to the fort and were surprised by the amount of activity going on.

There were people everywhere, including a few soldiers here and there. Susan hoped they hadn't bought out the store. They entered the large building, and she was pleasantly surprised by the amount of items for sale. Everything from baking goods to buffalo hides. She immediately saw the yarn she was looking for and parted from the group. The yarn looked to be good quality, and she immediately went to the sale counter.

"Lookin' to trade, miss?" A young man asked from behind the counter.

"Yes, I have clothes I can trade for yarn and knitting needles." She placed the clothes on the counter.

The young man immediately looked through the pile and nodded. "These are in good condition. I'll be able to sell them." He studied her for a moment before he smiled. "Come on lets figure out how much yarn you'll be needing." He stepped from behind the counter and escorted her to the yarn. "I don't have much in the way of colors."

"I was hoping for black with a bit of the natural color."

He grabbed a bunch of skeins, a pair of needles and carried them to the counter. He put them in a crate before she had a chance to say a word.

"Now, this should be enough to make yourself a blanket and a hat. Perhaps some socks too. If you need anything else ask for me. My name is Spud. Don't ask, it's a long story. You're a shrewd trader miss. Will you be at the dance tonight?"

"I haven't heard of any dance, Mr. Spud."

"It's just Spud. There's always a dance going on. Just follow the music after supper. I hope you'll save a dance for me."

Her face heated. "I will do that. Thank you." She grabbed the crate and walked out of the store. The fresh air felt good as she waited for her friends.

Two Army soldiers approached her. "Is your name Susan Farr?" The taller of the two asked.

"It was. I'm Susan Willis now. What's this all about?"

"Ma'am you'll need to come with us. Captain White would like to see you." The shorter one gestured with his hand for her to walk in front of him. "His office is the first door there."

The tall soldier opened the door for her and took the crate from her. Something wasn't right but what could she do? She needed to hear what the captain had to say.

The man behind the desk stood when she entered. His uniform was nicely pressed, and his dark hair was cut short. His gray eyes appeared to be a bit piercing as he looked her up and down. "Please have a seat." He waited until she sat in the wooden chair before he sat back down.

"I don't understand why I'm here." He did not look at all friendly.

"I received a telegram concerning you. There is the matter of a horse you stole. Now horse theft is a serious offense, you know. I've been instructed to take the horse from you."

"A horse? Do you mean Sunshine?"

"Miss Farr, if Sunshine is a bay, then yes." He folded his hands on his desk.

"My name is now Willis, Susan Willis. My husband sold Sunshine."

"I'll need to speak with your husband."

"I'm afraid that won't be possible. My husband is dead." She stood. "If that is all—"

"Mrs. Willis please sit back down. Now my cousin didn't mention a husband in his missive." He shook his head. "He said you stole the horse."

"And what? You plan to hang me?" She gave him her best stare. "Sunshine was my horse. If by cousin you mean the town banker, then he might see it differently. My parents died, and he ordered me to leave the house I was born in. I rode my horse to Independence. Upon my marriage my property became my husband's."

There was a knock on the door.

"Private, open the door." Captain White sat and waited for the door to open.

Relief ran through her at the sight of Mike.

"Are you all right?" Mike asked walking in without being invited. "What's going on here?"

The captain stood. "You sir, who might you be?"

"I'm Mike Todd, wagon master of the train Mrs. Willis is traveling with. She is under my protection. I'll ask again. What is this all about?" Mike's face looked fierce, and she was glad he was on her side.

"I'm inquiring about a horse that was in Mrs. Willis' possession. I have it on good authority it was stolen."

Mike laughed. "You mean Sunshine? Listen sir, that horse's only value was that it belonged to Mrs. Willis. The horse meant something to her. I bet that horse is still in Independence, unless it was sold to some unsuspecting soul."

Captain White's face grew red. "Justice needs to be served. She stole the horse, and she needs to repay the real owner. Mr. Benton is the real owner."

Mike looked at her with questions in his eyes.

"Mr. Benton is banker in the town where I grew up. He told me my father had mortgaged the farm, but it wasn't true. But he had papers with someone's signature on it. It wasn't my father's. I knew I had to leave. Mr. Benton was widely known for hurting people who crossed him." Her voice began to wobble.

"How much?" Mike asked his voice full or anger.

The officer came from the back of his desk and leaned casually against the front of it. His gaze raked over her and she felt dirty somehow. "You say she is under your protection. She could just as easily be under my protection."

Susan stood. "None of this makes sense. Why would Mr. Benton bother with me? He owns most of the town. One horse wouldn't make a difference to him. You can't keep me here."

"Yes I can. But you do have a choice. Your father had a lawyer friend with connections. He's claiming the signature on the mortgage papers was forged. Mr. Benton wants you to state in writing that it is in fact the signature of your father."

Mike cleared his throat. "Let me get this straight. The horse is of no consequence?"

"None whatsoever. I'm supposed to procure her statement. Then she's free to go."

Mike reached out and took her hand. "Let's go. We'll let you know what Mrs. Willis decides."

Her eyes widened and unease filled her but she did as Mike bade. She just hoped she wasn't shot in the back trying to leave.

"Your party won't be allowed to leave until I have the signature." Captain White glowered at them.

"Understood." Mike whisked her out the door but she turned back and grabbed her crate. Then she followed him across the Fort. Her hands shook so hard she thought she'd drop the crate and was grateful when Mike took it from her.

"What am I going to do?"

"He's just a captain. He's not in charge around here. Let's go back to our party and figure out our next move."

His confidence bolstered her spirits and gave her strength. Once again, he had come to her rescue.

CHAPTER EIGHT

ike watched Susan as she took in everyone's advice. The Motts offered to hide her, and Smitty offered to take off with her right then and there. Mike already knew what the remedy would be, but he wasn't sure what she'd think about it. She wouldn't be happy. He'd wait for Eli to get back with the information he'd asked him to gather.

He excused himself from their group as soon as he spotted his brother. Eli was smiling and Mike took that as a good sign.

"You were right, Mike. That captain doesn't have the authority to do anything. I talked to Colonel Newton. Now here's the bargain we struck. You and Susan marry up, and we can be on our way in the morning."

Mike's jaw dropped as his heart sped up. "What do you mean marry up?" He furrowed his brow.

"The captain might not have the authority, but he has connections. We'd end up either having to leave her behind or delay our trek to Oregon. The way I see it, we don't want to delay the trip." Eli smiled again.

"You're having fun at my expense aren't you? What did the colonel really say?" He rubbed the back of his neck as he stared at his brother.

"I'm smiling because I think you two would make a great couple. I see how you sneak looks at her. You don't think anyone else is watching but I am. I'd be happy to be your best man."

Mike wanted to smack the grin right off Eli's face. "I have no plans to tie myself down to a wife, pretty or not. Why I'd rather—"

"I didn't see you standing there, Susan. Did you see her, Mike? Because I didn't." Eli turned red and then he turned and went back to their wagon.

Susan stared at Mike with wide trusting eyes. He inwardly groaned. "Eli found a solution. I'm just not sure it's the right solution."

"What is it?" She had her bottom lip between her red lips.

"Well, you see. The Captain White has connections and can make this go the hard way. He could still claim horse theft. The Colonel Newton says we can either get married and be on our way or you have to stay. It would mean leaving you behind. We couldn't possibly lose so many days. We need to be through the south pass before winter hits, and that could be as early as September."

She clasped her hands in front of her and stared at the ground. "I see. What about the farm? If I stay, do I get to keep it?"

"Honey, I doubt you'll be able to keep it any which way you go with this thing."

She glanced up at him. "I'll do the sensible thing. I'll sign the paper and we'll go."

"Let me go and see what they have to say. I'm afraid if I take you inside the Fort, they'll arrest you. I don't understand why my marrying you would make much of a difference."

"I know you don't want to get married. Don't worry I won't tie you down but it is nice to know you think I'm pretty. I'll be waiting for your return." She walked back to the group before he had a chance to say another word.

Mike marched off in search of the Colonel Newton. Conveniently, he found both him and the captain walking together on the wooden walk in front of their offices. "Gentlemen, I think we have some business to discuss." He offered his hand to the Colonel.

The balding man shook Mike's hand. "You must be Mike Todd. I'm Colonel Newton. Captain White and I were just talking about your situation. Unfortunately, we'll need to confirm her identity before she can sign the papers. I sent a telegram to White's cousin. He has dropped the horse theft charge and has instructed us to keep Miss Farr here until he can send someone to witness the papers being signed."

"She shouldn't have to sign her home over," Mike contested.

"I agree. Unfortunately, people with money tend to get what they want. Now if you were to marry her, the property becomes yours and you can sign it over. I know of you and your reputation and we have plenty of witnesses to attest to your identity. That would be good enough for the captain's cousin."

"She's recently widowed. She's not looking to get married again so soon. Everyone in my party knows who she is."

White raised one eyebrow. "Oh? Does she have identification on her?"

Mike shook his head. "Most people don't. I'm just not sure you can do this."

The colonel sighed. "It's up to her. She's welcome to stay and wait, but I don't see the advantage to doing so. I wish things were fair but Mr. Todd you must know how things work in this world of ours."

Mike swallowed hard and nodded. "I'll go talk to her."

"I'll send the chaplain over in about an hour. You can come back with him and sign the papers. Tell the widow I'm sorry I couldn't do more for her." He shook Mike's hand.

What was he going to tell Susan? Heck, neither of them wanted to be married. She planned on being free when she got to Oregon. Clancy had promised her an annulment. Perhaps he could do the same. He wasn't quite sure how a man asked for an almost marriage. He'd do it so she could continue on with them but like he told Eli, he wasn't ready to settle down. He ran his fingers through his hair and tried to smile when he spotted Susan watching him.

She hurried over. "Well?"

His heart dropped. She had expected him to fix it. Instead, they were going to have to marry. He stared at her for a moment then took her hand. He led her behind his wagon and turned her to face him. "I tried, but it looks as though we're getting married in about an hour."

He knew she didn't want to get married, but he hadn't realized how repulsive the idea was to her. From the look of shock on her face, repulsive might be an underestimation.

"Look, we'll get married. You can stay in your wagon. Nothing has to change." Tears filled her eyes, and he wiped them away with the pad of his thumb before they had a chance to fall. "Being married to me is that objectionable?" he asked in a whisper.

She shook her head. "It's not that. This will be my second marriage to a man who doesn't really want nor need a wife. I appreciate you doing this, but I can just…"

"No, honey, we'll do this and be on our way again tomorrow."

"But why? Why do we need to get married?"

"It's the property. Either you stay until the man that

Banker is sending to identify you comes, or I sign the property over as your husband."

"I still don't understand. Why you?"

"I'm known around these parts. I've led parties the last four years, and people recognize me. I hate that you'll lose your farm."

She managed a glimmer of a smile. "I thought it was gone already. Thank you for helping me."

Their gazes met and held. Something passed between them, and he felt an instant bond with her. He wished they'd met in a different time. They probably would have been well matched. "The chaplain will be here in an hour, and then I go back to the fort and sign the papers. Oh, and no more stealing horses." He smiled at her.

Susan nodded. "I'd best go fix my hair. After all, I'm getting married."

He watched her walk away and felt lucky and sad at the same time. Lucky to have her in his life but sad it would never be more. It couldn't be.

SUSAN SAT in her wagon stunned. *Married?* Her chest tightened, and she had a hard time breathing. *My word! How?* She grabbed her hairbrush and held it close. *Did he even like her?*

She couldn't keep marrying men because it would benefit her. It simply wasn't right. Mike didn't want a wife, but he hadn't mentioned an annulment either.

"Susan, can I come in?" Natalie's calm voice was a welcome sound.

"Please do."

Natalie climbed into the wagon and sat down next to Susan. "My dear, you are very pale." She reached out and took her hand. "Susan you're shaking. Mike told me about the wedding. I thought I'd come and give you a hand getting ready."

"He doesn't love me. He doesn't even want a wife. I cause problems everywhere I go. Mike shouldn't marry me just to help me out. What if he meets the woman he's meant to be with and he's married to me? I could ruin his whole life."

Natalie gently took the hairbrush and started brushing Susan's hair. "I think Mike is a kind and very handsome man. He'll treat you right. You won't have to worry about him mistreating you."

"He is a good man, and he shouldn't tie himself to me. This is all happening because of greed. The banker, Mr. Benton, wants my family farm. He told me it was already his. That's why I left and went to Independence. It's a big mess, all for a piece of land."

"Hand me your hair pins. Mike told the rest of the wagon train you are marrying now because there is a chaplain. Some think it's romantic and there are a few that think it's too soon after Clancy's death. So, let's get your best dress on and have a wedding." Natalie finished Susan's hair.

"You're right. Let me get my dress. It's probably a bit wrinkled. I don't want to shame Mike if you already told the group."

"Susan are you almost ready?" Savanna called. "The chaplain is here."

Susan took a deep breath. "I'll be right out." She put on the dress and took a deep breath. "Natalie will you stand up with me?"

Natalie smiled. "I'd be proud to be your Matron of honor. Let's not leave your groom standing all by himself."

Susan nodded her gratitude. During her last marriage she'd been without a single friend. Her last marriage. It really was scandalous to marry so soon after Clancy's death, and she'd be getting the look of the devil from some of the women. She wasn't doing anything but trying to make it to Oregon and start a new life. Was that so bad?

She climbed out of the wagon and smoothed out her good dress. It would have to do. Lily raced toward her with a bouquet of wildflowers in her hand.

"These are for you on your special day!" Her eyes sparkled when she handed the ragged blossoms to Susan.

Susan took the flowers and then leaned down and hugged Lily. "It is a special day, isn't it? Let's go and find Mike." She tried to make her voice light and carefree but she failed. Her nerves began to get the better of her and she wanted to turn around and walk far into the woods. Life would be so simple if not for the interference of others. No person could be a complete hermit.

The Todd brothers all stood in front of a short stocky young man she assumed was the chaplain. Smitty was there too, with his hair all slicked down. But Susan only had eyes for Mike. He stood head and shoulders above the rest. He was far too good for her. Everyone liked him, and he was kind and fair and knowledgeable. People respected him, and he was so very handsome. He turned and looked at her. His blue eyes were full of happiness, and she wished it was directed toward her but she knew better. His broad shoulders, strong jaw and full lips kept her rapt attention.

It was a few moments before she became aware of the crowd waiting for her. Lily ran to where Natalie stood before the chaplain. This time Susan's smile was real. She had a serene feeling inside of her that told her everything was going to be all right. Clarke approached her and offered his arm. Her eyes misted as she realized his intent in giving her away.

"Ready?" he asked.

"Yes." She wasn't aware of how long the walk was. All she saw was Mike standing there waiting for her. Her heart thumped increasingly faster with each step she and Clarke took. Was this really the right thing to do? She almost turned around. Mike didn't deserve to be saddled with her but she couldn't shame him by leaving him standing there.

She couldn't deny the romantic dream she had of Mike loving her someday. Such things led to heartache, and she tried to be practicable, but times like this her heart overruled her head. Certainly, she could allow herself to dream for a few hours?

Clarke kissed her cheek and put her hand in Mike's. An explosion of awareness rushed through her at Mike's touch, and by the way his eyes flared she knew he'd felt it too. The chaplain seemed to go on and on and finally he announced them man and wife. Before she had a moment to think, Mike swooped down and kissed her.

It was a kiss better than anything she ever could have imagined. His masculine lips softened against hers, and she swore she heard his heart cry out to hers. Being in his arms felt so right, so pleasurable. It was like a homecoming and her heart felt so full it might burst. When the kiss ended, she stared at him, dazed. Her knees were weak, and she held on to him for a minute.

"Got your dancing shoes on?" Jed asked Mike when the first strains of a fiddle were played.

"You know I don't like to dance." Mike glanced at her. "But of course I'll dance at my wedding. Just as soon as I take care of business at the fort. Chaplain, I'll walk you back." He reached for her hand and gave it a gentle squeeze. "Save the first dance for me." He dropped her hand, and she watched both him and the chaplain walk to the ferry. She swallowed hard, remembering the reason for the wedding.

"Congratulations!" Savanna said giving her a hug. "You got yourself a wonderful husband."

"Thank you." She scanned the crowd. Most looked to be

happy for her but there was that same old group of women who acted as though she was no better than the mud on their shoes. It didn't really matter. She sighed, *wishing* it didn't matter. And maybe, for just a little while, it didn't have to. Pulling her shoulders back, she stood straight and proud, and then she put a smile on her face. It was their wedding day, and no one outside her circle of friends needed to know the full story.

"It's so romantic!" Lily said as she twirled in a circle. "I'm going to marry Jed when I get older."

"He's a good man," Susan replied.

"He's the handsomest man I've ever seen, and he had peppermint candies in his pocket."

"Shh, don't give away all my secrets," Jed said as he handed Lily a piece of candy. "Welcome to the family." He leaned down and kissed Susan on the cheek.

"Yes, welcome," Eli echoed. "Now, Mike pretends he doesn't want to dance, but it's his heart's desire." His eyes twinkled.

"I'll find out when he gets back. I have a feeling it's a joke between you brothers." Her smile almost faltered when she saw Bart staring at her intently. She'd hoped he'd decided to leave her alone. What was it he really wanted?

"Congratulations, Mrs. Todd." Susan turned and there was Nellie Walton standing with her hands over her stomach.

"Thank you. I'm glad you were here."

"Where did Mike go? He practically ran away after the vows were said."

Susan stiffened. "He's a gentleman. He escorted the Chaplain back to the Fort. His kindness and thoughtfulness is why I married him. He'll be back in no time." It was hard to keep her smile intact.

"I'm sure he will." Nellie hurried off toward the bunch of

old hens that apparently sent her over to find out what she could.

"Deep breaths, dear," Savanna said. "They're just jealous. Mike is a fine-looking man. I bet they all had their eye on him."

"What shall we do while we wait for Mike to come back. I can't just stand here while everyone stares at me."

Savanna nodded. "We move Mike's things into your wagon of course. Smitty is packing for him right now. All you have to do is supervise where he should put them. That should keep the biddies busy. Your real friends stand with you, Susan."

Susan took Savanna's hand and squeezed it. "I know and it means everything to me. It's a blessing to have real friends. People like you and Clarke aren't easy to find."

"Come on before you make me cry. We're happy to have you as part of our family."

IMPATIENT WASN'T a strong enough word for what Mike was feeling. It was taking forever to get the papers all signed and witnessed. He needed to get back and put up a good united front with Susan. His heart warmed. Who was he kidding? He just wanted to be near her. She somehow made him want to be a better person.

The air in Colonel Newton's office was stuffy, and when their business was done, Mike shook the officer's hand and hightailed it out of Fort Laramie. Usually he enjoyed stopping at the fort but this time he wanted it far behind him. The lengths people went to in the name of greed never stopped astounding him.

He rounded the wagon at the rear and there was Susan. Did she have any idea how lovely she was? Her inner beauty radiated and enhanced her outer loveliness. She never put on airs. She was genuine and sweet… His footsteps faltered. He gave himself a mental shake. No, stop! He couldn't think that way. Bittersweet regret filled him. She was a once in a lifetime woman and he would have to let her go at the end of the trip.

She glanced up, and her smile grew wide when their gazes collided. How was he going to resist her? Movement to her right drew his attention to his brothers. Eli said something and laughed, and Jed aimed a light punch at his shoulder. A lump formed in his throat. He'd decided long ago that his life would be spent protecting and teaching his brothers. His plans didn't include a family of his own. It was a sacrifice he willingly made. He swallowed hard. Until now.

Lengthening his stride, he was at her side in no time. "It's all taken care of. You are no longer a wanted woman."

Her sigh of relief was loud. "Thank you. Smitty packed your things, and your brothers put them in my wagon. I know it's not what you want." She stared into his eyes, and he knew the answer she was looking for, but he just couldn't.

"It'll be fine. As long as we have the illusion of a happy marriage, I think we'll be fine. People will leave you be soon enough."

Her smile started to wither, but then she regained it. "Of course. We'll play along for a while. Speaking of which, I do believe we have some dancing to do in a bit. Your brothers have assured me that dancing is your most favorite thing to do." She laughed.

"They told you that did they? Troublemakers the both of them." He laughed with her. There was nothing wrong with being good friends.

The first strains of fiddle music cut through the air as someone started playing, and in short order a banjo and a harmonica filled out the sound. Mike held out his hand to

Susan. Her hand trembled a bit, and he gave her what he hoped was a reassuring smile. He led her into the middle of the circle the party made and he pulled her into his arms. He wanted to groan out loud at the rightness of having her there. She lit a fire inside him and he never wanted to let her go.

As he looked out at the crowd, he saw more smiles than frowns. People were happy for them, and he hoped eventually the group of harpies would die off. The glare Bart threw his way gave him pause. He'd need to keep an eye on that man.

Two by two, other dancers joined them. At the tap on his shoulder, he turned to discover a grinning Smitty cutting in on him. The big man took Susan with him around the dance floor. Mike hoped to escape, but he ended up dancing with just about every woman in camp. Eli and Jed had pointed and laughed at first, but now they appeared grim as they too danced.

Finally, He got close enough to reclaim Susan. "Had enough?"

"For now. I need some water. Dancing is thirsty work."

He led her to their wagon, filled the dipper with water, and offered it to her. She took it and drank. "Thank you. My toes hurt. Most of the men aren't as fine a dancer as you are."

He couldn't stop the smile tugging on his lips. "So you think I'm a fine dancer?"

A becoming blush spread over her cheeks, and he was sorry he teased her. He needed to keep his distance, but instead he'd been getting closer than ever. Mike took the dipper from her and refilled it for himself. He really needed to pour the water on his head to cool himself down, but he drank it down. He sipped, placing his lips in the same spot she had, and his heart thudded heavily in his chest.

"About the sleeping arrangements. It'll look odd if I sleep

under the wagon. I think I'll take guard duty tonight. I don't want you to be uncomfortable."

She shook her head. "Mike, you most certainly will not be on guard duty on our wedding night. She put her hands on her hips. "We've waited a long time to be together, and now we can. You'll sleep with me."

His eyes widened as she put her hands around his neck and pulled him down for a hug.

"The Sugartons are watching us," she whispered.

He moved his head to look, but all he could focus on were her ripe red lips. Before he could stop himself, he was kissing her. He forgot they were being watched. Nothing mattered except for the feel of her lips under his. He cradled her cheeks in his hands when he pulled away to look at her.

She broke off her gaze and stepped back. Her eyes were full of doubt, and he couldn't blame her. He fought his feelings, but he didn't want to mislead her.

"They're gone. I'll stay on my side of the wagon. You'll have no need to worry."

The flicker of light in her eyes dimmed. "That sounds like a fine idea. I'm going to say goodnight to a few people then I'll get into bed. I have to warn you there isn't a lot of room in the wagon, but I think we'll manage."

He nodded and watched as she hurried off. There was nothing else he could do. Guard duty would have been a heck of a lot easier than spending the night with constant temptation. He'd best see to shutting down the camp. Maybe he could walk himself tired enough not to care.

Stillness blanketed the camp when he returned to the wagon. After a few sidelong glances from some of the men in his care that told him they thought he was crazy for not starting his wedding night, he'd had little choice but to return. Silence came from the wagon. Hopefully, Susan had fallen asleep. He eased his way inside. She hadn't been wrong about the space inside. Though she'd loaded her items neatly, he still had trouble maneuvering around them. She lay on her right side, facing the wood and canvas. She'd left an open spot behind her, but it was going to be tight. He eased his body down and found not an inch to spare. There was no help for it, he had to lie against her.

Her warmth and softness seemed to melt against him. Her scent tantalized. Desire rose within him, and his throat went dry. It was going to be a long, *long* night.

CHAPTER NINE

Susan admired the view as she drove the wagon. Since leaving Fort Laramie, mountains had risen in the distance ahead. It seemed as though the plains were behind them. The rolling hills were lovely, and the mountains gave her much to ponder. Mike had announced that it would be more difficult from here on out, and by the look of the craggy landscape, she was certain his words rang true.

Gazing toward the head of the wagon train, she caught sight of her handsome husband. They'd been married over a week now, and she'd spent many hours uncertain. How was she supposed to act toward him? He was contrary for a man. One minute he liked her smile, the next he didn't. One minute he enjoyed her company, and then abruptly he'd get up and leave. He was a restless sleeper, and in the small space, his every toss disturbed her rest. She was becoming exhausted from a lack of sleep.

She never complained, and she tried to keep a smile on her face, but it was becoming increasingly difficult. With every frown he sent in her direction, she felt as though she didn't measure up to his idea of a wife. They really weren't husband and wife, and it shouldn't have mattered if he was pleased with her or not, but it did matter. It mattered a lot.

The group of gossipy hens watched them constantly. It was disheartening. Natalie and Savanna told her to ignore them but for some reason she found that near impossible. Their stares of doubt and disapproval lingered in her heart no matter how much she told herself to pay no heed.

The signal came for them to halt for the noon meal. She scrambled down off the wagon and began to tend to the oxen. Mike was immediately at her side.

"How are you today?" he asked.

"I'm fine. I'll have food ready for you in no time. You know I can do this all myself. You have everyone else in the company to help too."

"I keep an eye on everyone." He took her hand and turned her until she faced him. He reached out with his free hand and ran the pad of his thumb under her eye. "You look so tired. You need to rest."

She closed her eyes for a moment. His touch sent shivers down her spine. "I'm fine, really I am. You don't need to worry about me. Besides you don't get much sleep yourself."

She heard a gasp and quickly turned. Connie Ranger stared at her with wide eyes. "Some things shouldn't be talked about." She turned and hurried away.

Mike's laughter started as a small rumble in his chest before it became loud. He had an infectious type of laughter, and she soon joined in. Still holding her hand, he pulled her into an embrace. Their laughter quieted as they gazed at one another. Anticipation filled her as she waited for him to kiss her. He gave her a peck on the forehead and stepped away from her.

It took everything she had to keep a smile on her face as she realized that was all she'd ever have from him. She'd known, but she'd hoped.

Lily ran over, her eyes full of excitement. "Susan, the ladies are all talking about taking baths in the river tonight. Jed said we'd be pulling away from the river soon enough. It'll be great fun!"

Susan nodded. "Sounds like fun."

"Of course you'll come with us won't you?"

"Yes, Lily, thank you for inviting me."

"I'm going to tell Savanna, bye." She ran off in the direction of the Mott wagon.

"Will we be moving away from the river?"

"We sure will. In the next few days, we'll stop an hour earlier than usual so clothes can be washed, barrels filled, and I know how you ladies like to be clean." Mike sat down on a crate and took the biscuits with jam Susan offered him.

"You know much about ladies do you?" she teased.

He straightened and sat up nice and tall as he looked into her eyes. "Just you. I don't need to know about anyone else."

Her heart pounded painfully against her chest. He obviously didn't know how his words affected her. She took too much to heart but she couldn't help it. "I'm complicated enough."

"Yes, you are." He finished eating and then he stood. "Get a bit of rest if you can. I'll take care of the oxen and the wagon. At least lay down for a bit."

It wasn't a bad idea, and she was tired. After putting the food away, she climbed into the back of the wagon and rested.

Susan opened her eyes. Someone was driving the wagon and not very smoothly. Her teeth gritted as the wheels went over bump after bump. *What in the world?* She quickly sat up and then got to her knees. She then crawled to the front and looked out. It was Mike driving, and she couldn't stop the warmth that filled her heart.

He turned his head and grinned at her. "Hello, sleepy one."

"Why didn't you wake me to drive? The others will think—"

"—that I'm your husband. I'm allowed to take care of you. Jed and Eli are riding up and down the line looking out for the others. Go and get more sleep if you like."

She scrambled out to the bench and sat next to Mike. "With the way you drive?"

Mike laughed. "And what is wrong with the way I drive?"

"I do believe you hit every bump on the trail. I'll be surprised if I'm not covered in bruises." She grinned back.

"I'd be happy to check for you. Roll up your sleeve and I'll check your arm." The teasing light in his eyes tugged at her heart and trapped the breath in her lungs.

"You have no sense of propriety. What will the—"

"—other's think?" Mike finished. "That, my dear, is your problem. You worry about what others think. There are always going to be people who think what you do is wrong or not up to their standards. Tell me, do those judgmental people look happy? Do they smile? Do they laugh? You've done nothing worth being looked down upon or talked about. People who love you and care about you like you just the way you are."

A great weight lifted from her shoulders. "You're right. Old habits are hard to break. My parents were always so concerned with what the neighbors or the town would think. Living that way does steal your happiness. It made me shy. I was always afraid I'd say or do the wrong thing and it's hard to live that way." Susan rolled up her sleeve and showed her arm to Mike. "No bruises, but I'm surprised." She laughed.

"See, you need to laugh more. It becomes you."

"I'm sure anything is better than my perpetual frown."

Mike shook his head. "You smile. I've seen you smile

often, in fact. It's one of the things I like best about you. Your smile lights up the whole sky." His smile faded and he turned his concentration to the trail.

Susan looked out at the mountains in the distance. He felt it too. He felt the pull between them. Her love for him grew, and she wanted to groan out loud. Love was a curse. In this case, it was the very worst curse. She wanted to be able to touch him and have him hold her. She wanted shared smiles and laughter. She wanted memories they would share forever together. She wanted to call him hers but he wasn't and he never would be. She'd take what she could she supposed and the memories would be hers alone.

LATER THAT DAY, Mike walked from Smitty's fire toward his and Susan's. It was bath night, and everyone was hurrying to get the food prepared so they could all go to the river. His chest tightened. Susan would smell even better afterwards, and he'd suffer for it. Her soap was lavender scented. If only he could hide it from her.

"Of course, you won't want to come with us tonight," Mike heard Trudy say. His hackles rose at the hint of challenge in her voice. "You'll want to be with your husband as a newlywed and all."

Upon rounding the wagon, he came upon Connie and Trudy, hemming Susan in against the back.

He slowly walked to Susan and wrapped his arm around her waist. "You two don't need to concern yourself with what my wife does. I hadn't thought of it, but I suppose you're right. What could be more romantic than a dip in the water under the moonlight?"

Connie and Trudy exchanged glances and frowned.

"Well, we just wanted your wife to know she wasn't invited," Connie said.

"Come now just because you're both jealous that Susan married the best man there ever was, is no reason to be hateful to her. Meanness doesn't look good on you."

Their eyes widened and then they turned and hurried away.

"The best man there ever was?" Susan laughed.

He shrugged his shoulders. "It's the truth and it made them leave."

She laughed even harder then abruptly stopped. "You're going to have to go to the river with me, you know."

"I have no problem with that. I won't peek, and I won't touch. I know how to be a gentleman." She looked into his eyes and nodded.

"We'll go after everyone else is finished."

"Sure, honey." He wanted to choke. How was he going to keep from peeking? "I need to talk to Jed about something. I'll be back." He took long strides to get away from her as quickly as possible. He'd have to find another way. He didn't have enough control to keep from touching her. He wanted her with everything within him. It was best to avoid temptation altogether.

Thankfully, he ran into Clarke, and when he explained his problem, Clarke agreed to guard Savanna, Susan, Natalie, and Lily. Clarke suggested having Savanna plan it. She usually got people to do as she asked.

Mike hadn't realized just how tense his body was until Clarke walked away. If things were different, nothing would have stopped him from taking Susan, but they were in an impossible situation. He knew her to be untouched, and she'd still be that way when they parted.

Later, he stopped by and told Susan he had to help fix a wagon, and he wouldn't be able to take her after all. She just nodded and told him of her plan to go with her friends. Now if he'd only been able to hide her sweet-smelling soap.

He didn't want to be a liar, so he did indeed help repair a few wagons. He'd just finished fixing a wheel when he heard the screams coming from the bathing area. His heart squeezed. Susan was by the river.

With Eli on his heels, Mike sprinted to the riverbank; both had their guns drawn. Savanna was trying to get to Susan who lay still on the opposite bank. Natalie stood in the water screaming with blood running down her face, and there was no sign of Lily. Clarke must have been knocked out, but he looked to be coming around.

Jed rode up on his horse took one look, crossed the river and gave chase. Mike's heart dropped into his stomach. Lily had been taken.

Mike got to Susan before Savanna and he let out a breath he didn't know he held. She didn't open her eyes, but she was alive. He scooped her up into his arms and offered his arm for Savanna to hold onto as he made his way to the bank. Clarke reached down and helped Savanna out of the water.

People came with guns and blankets. Eli carried Natalie out of the water and handed her off to Smitty.

"Indians stole my baby," Natalie cried. "My Lily. My sweet, sweet Lily is gone." She wailed as she wept. Smitty carried her to his fire, wrapped a blanket around her wet chemise, and sat her down. He then laid a blanket on the ground and helped Mike lay Susan on it before he covered her with another blanket.

"There were two of them," Savanna said. She stood in the circle of Clarke's arms, shivering. Nellie Walton ran forward with a quilt and handed it to Clarke. "They were there before we knew it. They hit Clarke then tried to drag Lily away. We tried to stop them. Susan fought and fought but they ended up stabbing her in the shoulder before one of them hit her in the back of her head. Natalie never gave up either, they hit her head, and she went down. I'm afraid I was useless. I wasn't close enough to try to grab her back." Savanna crumpled to the ground and cried. Clarke sat down and pulled her onto his lap. Blood ran down the side of his face.

Mike quickly rolled Susan onto her side and checked her shoulder. Sure enough, she'd been stabbed. A quick glance down revealed a fair amount of blood on his clothes.

Smitty grabbed medical supplies from the back of the wagon and edged Mike out of the way. "Let me check it out. She'll need some sewing, I bet."

Mike jumped up. "Smitty, you're in charge. Eli and I will go after Lily."

"Mike, you can't leave. You're the captain," Smitty said.

"I'll go," Ranger said, taking a step forward. "I can track. All I ask is that you look after Connie for me."

Connie gasped and grabbed her father's arm. "You can't leave me."

"You'll be in good hands. Don't you worry." He gently pried her hand off his arm.

"Done," said Smitty. "Grab your guns and ammo; I'll gather some supplies for you."

Max stepped forward. He was a big man dressed in buck-skins who Bart had hired on at Fort Laramie to help drive his wagon. "I know this country pretty well. I'd like to go and look for her too."

Mike furrowed his brow. He would have sworn any friend of Bart's was going to be trouble but it didn't seem to be the case. "I'd appreciate that, Max."

Mike walked with Eli toward the horses. "Eli, find Jed. If you can't locate her in a few days you need to come back. You know the trail we'll be on." He lowered his voice. "I hate to say this, but it's likely she's already dead."

Eli nodded. "I know but we need to try to find her. We might just get lucky."

"I hope so." Mike hugged his brother and then shook Ranger's hand. "Thanks for stepping up, Ranger."

"We'll give it our best shot, but you know how Indian abductions usually go. Take care of my girl."

"Will do." Mike watched them mount up and ride away. He could only pray they'd find Lily quickly and in one piece.

When he returned to the fire, he was heartened to see Susan's eyes open. She still lay on the ground, and her face was deathly pale. She reached out toward him with her right arm, and he immediately went to her. Holding her hand, he sat down next to her and brushed her hair back from her face. Smitty had stitched her up, but blood was already seeping through the bandage.

"I tried. Really, I tried. I hit one of them with a rock and cut his leg. He stabbed me and when I tried to hit him again, he hit me in the head. Lily is gone." Tears poured down her face as she stared into his eyes.

"I know, sweetheart, I know. You were very brave." An image of Susan being the one taken flashed through his mind, and his heart raced. A lump formed in his throat as he gazed down at his wife. *What if it had been her?*

"I need to talk to the men about guard duty and see who will drive yours, Natalie's and Connie's wagons."

"Natalie and I can drive one together. It'll keep her busy."

He shook his head. "You're in no condition to hold the oxen in line."

"I won't actually drive. I'll sit next to Natalie and keep her from falling apart." Her eyes held a silent plea, and after a moment he nodded.

"I'll talk to her about it. It'll only take me a moment, and I'll get you into dry clothes." He stood and started to walk toward a group of men when he realized what he'd just said.

He changed direction and went over to the O'Leary family. They usually kept to themselves but Mrs. O'Leary was the mothering type.

"Mr. O'Leary, Mrs. O'Leary," he greeted.

"What can we do for you, Captain?" Mr. O'Leary stepped forward and shook Mike's hand.

"I was hoping Mrs. O'Leary could help my wife change into dry clothes." He felt his face warm at the couple's perusal.

Mrs. O'Leary bit back a smile. "I'd be happy to. Harvey here will help me get her into your wagon. You won't be gone long, will ya?"

"I'll be there in a bit. Thank you so much." He tipped his hat before he turned and walked toward the other men.

Susan lay comfortably in the wagon. She had clean dry clothes on, and Smitty had given her something for the pain. The Indian had meant to kill her and it shook her to her core. Lily's scream echoed in her head. What was happening to her? And poor Natalie. Her cries could be heard throughout the camp. It broke Susan's heart.

The wagon rocked, and she grabbed for her loaded musket. Sitting up, she aimed it.

"It's me!"

She sagged against the side of the wagon and closed her eyes. "I could have shot you."

Mike took the gun out of her hands. "Good thing you didn't." He set the firearm to the side and lay down beside her. Leaning up on his elbow he looked her over. "Are you alright? What about your shoulder? How's your head?"

His concern warmed her. "I'm not worried about myself. I keep reliving the moments at the river. They had no interest in the rest of us. They only wanted Lily. Why do you suppose that is?"

"She's young. How old is she?"

"Thirteen I think. They wouldn't..."

Mike shook his head. "The younger ones are usually made part of the tribe. Part of their family. Though they do tend to marry younger than we do."

"Marry?" She couldn't contain the horror in her voice.

"I shouldn't have said anything. The truth is I have no idea why they took her. Jed left hot on their trail. I'm hoping he can get her back." He reached down and touched her face.

A sharp ache lanced through her temple, and she hissed through her teeth.

"Sorry," he murmured, withdrawing his hand. "That's a bad bruise, and your face is going to be swollen for a while."

But she didn't care about that. "Jed and Eli are both in danger aren't they? If only we hadn't gone to the river." Tears spilled over and rolled down her face.

"They've probably been watching us for a while. I should have noticed at some point. You can't blame yourself. There is so much out here that can hurt you. We can only try our best to get to Oregon in one piece."

She dashed her tears away with her hands. "You do this over and over. Aren't you afraid?"

He rolled onto his back and gently eased her body so her head lay on his chest. "Of course I'm afraid. But it's what we do. Eli, Jed, Smitty, and I all chose to be guides. There is danger, but there's also great satisfaction in leading those who need us."

She could hear his heart beating as she lay against him. With him, she was safe and warm. She moved a bit and his arms tightened around her. "I thought you'd fallen asleep," she whispered.

"No, too much on my mind. I could have lost you today,

and my mind won't let go of the possible sorrow I would have felt. You've come to mean a lot to me." His voice grew husky.

Not knowing what to say, she swallowed hard and nodded. Parting in Oregon was going to be even harder than she'd thought. Not wanting the closeness to end, she stayed still, enjoying the warmth of his hard body. He stroked her hair, and it was heavenly.

Morning came far too soon, and he eased her back to her side of the wagon. "I'll grab us some food. I don't want you doing much today. Are you in pain?"

"A bit. Could you ask Smitty for some of his special tea? And I need to check on Natalie."

"Let me get out, and I'll lift you down. I mean it. I want you to take it easy." He stared at her long and hard until she nodded in agreement.

She was glad she'd had Mrs. O'Leary dress her in clothes instead of a nightgown. Grabbing her hairbrush and hair pins, she bit back a smile. She was excited to have Mike's hands around her waist. She couldn't fight her feelings anymore, and if she'd learned anything on her journey west, it was that life was unpredictable.

She sat at the fire Mike had made for her and struggled through her pain to put her hair up. She felt someone staring at her and sure enough when she looked up, there was Big Bart. That was it! She'd had enough.

"What is it you want? I feel as though you are keeping an eye on me."

He cocked his right brow. "I need your wagon. My oxen are getting weak, and I need to lighten the load of my wagon. It is my wagon after all." He strolled in her direction as he talked.

"It now belongs to my husband. You have no business with me. Besides, I need the wagon for my things. You may have to leave some of your things on the side of the trail. We've passed many items the last few days."

"You don't want to pay the price of my anger. I owe both you and the wagon, and I aim to collect." He glared at her.

A chill filled her. "You might as well try to strike a deal with someone else. Like I said, all my worldly possessions now belong to Mike."

"Have you gotten rid of Clancy's things? You could make room in your wagon if you threw his things out."

She stood and put her hands on her hips. "I gave his things to people who had use for them. I still have no room for your things." She wasn't about to tell him she traded many of Clancy's things at Fort Laramie. He might insist everything she got in trade belonged to him. She widened her eyes. "It's whiskey isn't it? Clancy promised to transport it for you?"

"A fair and right woman would honor her dead husband's wishes," Bart snarled.

"I never said I was fair and right, Mr. Bigelow. I'll have to ask you to leave my fire. You're making my head ache something awful."

"This isn't the end."

She sighed when he left. She was sure it wasn't the end too.

"What was that all about?" Mike asked. He handed her a cup of tea and set a plate of eggs and biscuits down on a crate.

"His oxen are tired of dragging his whiskey across the world. He still insists that my wagon belongs to him. He still thinks I belong to him too. He has some nerve. I told him that everything now belongs to you."

"Gee, thanks." Mike chuckled. "Don't let him worry you. He'll just have to leave some of his precious whiskey behind. I have drivers for all the wagons. Natalie insists on driving and having you with her. Clarke and Savanna are in good shape, and I found a young fella to drive Connie's rig."

"How young?"

"Young enough she won't spend her day distracting him. That girl sure does like to flirt." He shook his head. "How about you? Will you be able to sit all day? I can manage to have you lay down in the wagon if you'd prefer."

"I'll let you know when we stop for the noon meal. Are you sure we have to go on? Maybe if we waited here, Lily would make it back."

"I wish we had the luxury of time, but we don't. Jed and Eli know the route we're taking. I have every confidence they'll meet up with us as soon as they know something." He leaned down and kissed her cheek. "Eat while it's still warm. I'll hitch up the wagons and then pack up."

His kiss calmed her. He was a confident man, with a steadying influence, and she liked that about him.

CHAPTER TEN

*T*hey made good time, and two days later they were about to leave the Platte river valley. Mike constantly searched the horizon for his brothers, Ranger and Max, but so far there was nothing. He rode up and down the train announcing that they were stopping for the day at noon. This would be the last chance for water and good grazing for the livestock for about a week. They were headed into a desert-like valley.

Although they passed many graves along the trail, they hadn't lost another soul. Now, if only the rescue party would return with Lily, things would be perfect. Natalie and Susan rode together, and Susan had a calming effect on Natalie, though she got awfully quiet when she was around him.

She woke several times each night from nightmares, and he did his best to make her feel safe. He held her through the night and it was getting harder and harder not to make her his wife in truth, but he couldn't take advantage of her. He wanted her with everything in him, and as difficult as it was, he wouldn't trade his nights with her for anything. She never complained, but he knew her shoulder was giving her the devil. She'd make someone one heck of a wife.

He ran his fingers through his hair. She would have made him one heck of a wife. But he didn't have a choice. What was he supposed to do? Stash her in Oregon for a few years until his guide days were behind him? He got down off Arrow and kicked at the dirt. He had too much to think about.

He hurried to Natalie's wagon and helped her off before he lifted Susan down. He allowed his hand to linger on her waist, and her responding blush made him feel ten feet high.

"This is our last chance for clean water and grass to graze for almost a week. Men will be accompanying the women to the river so they can get water, wash clothes, and whatever else is needed. Don't go unescorted."

"We're the last people you need to give warning to," Natalie said sadly.

"I know, and I'm sorry. My brothers and Ranger will be back any day now."

Natalie crossed her arms in front of her. "How do you know they aren't already dead?"

Susan gasped.

"I'd know if they were dead."

"How? How do you know it?" Natalie demanded.

"I'd feel their loss in my heart. It's always been that way between us. We seem to know when one of us is in trouble. I can just feel it is all."

"Do you think as a mother I'd know if my Lily was dead?" Her look of hope almost broke his heart.

"It's possible."

Susan put her arm around Natalie's waist. "Yes, there is always hope. Mike, what about trees? Will there be firewood in the next part of our journey?"

"Not much, if any. You'll have to collect Buffalo chips. It'll be fine. Just remember not to drink any of the groundwater until we get to Willow Spring. I need to make the rounds." He smiled at Susan. "I'll be back in a bit if you need to get water."

He took care of the oxen first, and then he walked from wagon to wagon, giving everyone the same do-not-drink-the-water speech. He helped repair a few of the wagons and advised others to grease their wagon wheels. He even filled a few water barrels for some. He made sure no one went to the river alone.

Still he searched the horizon for his brothers. The young man, Peter, was a great help to Connie Ranger, and she seemed content for the moment. Mike finally made it to Smitty's fire and poured himself a cup of coffee. A look of understanding was exchanged.

"They'll be back soon, Mike. You just wait and see," Smitty told him as he nodded firmly.

"I know, but that doesn't stop the worrying. I keep telling myself Eli is seventeen and Jed is fifteen, practically men, but we've been looking out for each other for a long time now."

"You sure have, and they can take care of themselves, thanks to you. I'm proud of you, Mike, and your parents would have been mighty proud too. You just wait. They'll be here soon."

"Thanks Smitty, that means a lot. I have to fill a few wash-tubs for Susan and Natalie. I don't want them going down to the river if they don't want to."

"Use my fire to heat water too."

Mike grinned. "Thanks Smitty." He walked around the outside of the wagons and saw Big Bart staring at Susan's rig. Anger filled him.

"See something you like?" Mike stood toe to toe with a surprised Bart.

"Looking out for my investment is all. I own that wagon,

and your wife belongs to me. I bought them both and I expect to have them."

Mike gave him a hard look. "We've been over this, Bart. You can't own a white woman—"

"I can if I have a contract for her services. I have a bill of sale for the wagon too, if you'd like to see them." Bart smiled widely.

"Why wait until now to show your hand?"

"I need the wagon, and I have an itch for your wife. Plus I hired Max to drive the wagon. When he returns I'm going to need the wagon. You're not the law, so you're not going to stop me."

"As far as this wagon train goes, I am the law. If you like we can take it to a vote." Mike said trying to keep his voice casual.

"Once they see the signed papers, they'll vote in my favor, guaranteed."

"I was talking about the vote whether we leave you behind or not." Mike gave him a lazy smile. "Think about it and get back to me."

Bart pulled a knife out of his belt, but the sound of a rifle cocking stilled him. He took his hand of the hilt of the knife and glared. "See you around." He backed up, turned, and walked away.

"He's one mean man," Smitty said.

"Thanks for having my back."

"No need for thanks. Your wife came and got me." Smitty nodded his head toward the left where Susan stood.

She stood looking as though the weight of the whole world was upon her. Mike opened his arms and she flew into them, holding onto him for all he was worth. He closed his eyes and cherished the feel of her against him. Somehow having her near him made the world brighter.

"What does he mean he has a contract? I'm scared, Mike.

He's always watching as though he's just waiting for the right moment. Part of Clancy's soul must have been black for him to do this."

He stroked her back. "You're right only if he did indeed do such a thing. Bart has been saving his proof all this time? Something isn't right."

"He did tell me his oxen were getting tired and he needed to put some of the things from his wagon into mine. I said no."

"We'll keep our eyes open. You need to be armed."

"I carry a knife. It's strapped to my thigh. Unfortunately, I took it off when we were in the river or I could have at least wounded one of those Indians."

He held her closer. "Thank God you didn't. You'd be dead for sure, and I don't want to think about a time without you." He became quiet. He'd already said too much, and he couldn't give her false hope.

NATALIE THREW a wet cloth across their camp. "I can't take this anymore. The waiting and wondering has been excruciating, and my heart is so broken. Why? Why did my husband have to go west? Did I ever tell you we left a prosperous farm for the unknown?" She crossed her arms in front of her and frowned. "'It'll be a great adventure,' he said. 'A chance of a lifetime.' Ha! His life was cut short, and now my Lily is out there with, those, those heathens. I can only imagine what they are doing to her. My poor, sweet, sweet girl." She sank down onto a crate and buried her face in her hands as she wept. "We keep going, and with every turn of the wheel we get farther away from my baby."

Susan put her hand on Natalie's shoulder. "I wish I had a way to make everything better, Natalie."

Natalie covered Susan's hand with hers. "I'd go crazy if not for you. I think these past days of nothing but white sand is making me mad. I worry we won't make it across without the oxen dying. People are starting to guard their water barrels and there is a feeling of unease."

"I know, I feel it too. Mike said we'd be clear of this alkaline torture by the end of the day tomorrow. Why don't you lie down and rest for a bit?"

"Sounds like a good idea, thank you Susan. You've been like a sister to me." Before Susan could reply, Natalie climbed into the wagon.

A *sister*. The words poured over her and warmed her heart. Some people actually liked her. She wasn't painted with a tainted brush to her friends here. Confidence filled her. She could do this. She could make this trip and be just fine. She'd doubted herself for so long, and those doubts were unwarranted.

A cloud of dust formed in the distance. Riders were coming, and she prayed it was Lily. She watched and waited. There were only four horses but that didn't mean Lily wasn't with them. She held her breath as they rode closer. No, Lily wasn't with them, and her heart dropped. After making sure Natalie was still sleeping, Susan hurried to where the rescue party was arriving.

They never did see Lily but they'd heard from a trapper that she was with a band of Sioux and she was being treated well. What did that even mean? Being treated well could really mean anything, but at least she was alive. Poor Natalie.

Mike ambled to her side and put his arm around her shoulder, pulling her close. "There isn't much we can do. We'll file a report, and the army will keep an eye out for her."

"They won't go looking for her?"

"Not necessarily. They don't like to tangle with the Sioux

if they don't have to. The Indians usually hide the white prisoners from the soldiers. The main thing is she's alive."

Susan snaked her arms around Mike's waist and held on to him. "At least you have your brothers back. I know that's a great relief to you."

"He glanced down at her upturned face and smiled. "I was starting to get worried. Jed seems to be taking it harder than most. I think he had a crush on Lily. She'll never be fit for a wife after living with the Indians. I know it sounds harsh, but it's true. Where's Natalie?"

"Taking a lay-down. This is going to break her heart. I don't know what she plans to do once we make it to Oregon." Her heart squeezed. She didn't know what she was going to do either. Would there be jobs? What about a place to live? She'd been a naive girl when she ran, married, and joined the train. Now she felt older, much older.

Mike kissed her right temple. "Let her sleep. She'll get the news soon enough. We'll make sure she's settled when she gets to Oregon. You don't need to worry. She'll be welcome to stay at the ranch. She'll be good company for you." He took a step away from her, and his lips formed a grim line, as though he'd just uttered words he'd never meant to say.

She simply nodded. It wasn't going to happen that way, and she knew it. They could stay a few days but then it would be time for her and Mike to part. Perhaps Natalie could work at the ranch, though. That would be a great opportunity for her. As for herself, she wouldn't be able to live near Mike and not be with him. Her heart was already vested, and she felt like a fool. It was too late now. She'd tried and tried to guard her heart to no avail. Every time she gazed at him, her stomach fluttered in the most unsettling way. His touch sent a series of explosions throughout her body.

She walked back to the wagon and started to make the meal, not that she had much of an appetite, and Natalie probably wouldn't eat either. The noise level in the wagon circle grew louder as everyone passed on the information that Lily hadn't been found, and Natalie was soon awake and stumbling out of the wagon.

"Is she dead? Oh my God, she's dead!" She swayed.

Susan placed her hands on Natalie's arms and steadied her. "Hush, she's not dead. There was a sighting of her. That's good news."

Natalie wrenched free and ran to the bushes to vomit.

Susan waited for the retching to stop and then went to her side with a wet cloth. "I'm so sorry. Of course it's not good news, but…"

Natalie washed her face and nodded. "I know what you mean. I think I'm going to go crazy. I imagine all kinds of horrible things happening to her. In my mind, everything I've ever heard about Indians and torture, well, it's all being done to her. I can't sleep, and my heart hurts so much. I've lost everyone, and now I'm alone. But as bad as it is for me, I just know it's so much worse for my Lily."

Susan put her arms around her friend and held her while she wept. It was a long time before Natalie quieted down enough for Susan to let her go. "Come, let's get you some coffee." She gently led her to the fire, sat her down on a crate, and handed her a cup of coffee.

"Big Bart approached me yesterday. He wants to put some of his things in my wagon. He told me Max would drive it. He also said he'd make sure I'd be cared for in Oregon." Natalie sighed and took a sip of her coffee.

Susan's jaw dropped. "He didn't! Why that lowdown snake! It's nothing but whiskey he needs to get to Oregon for his saloon, and I bet he plans for you to work there. That was his plan for me. Somehow, Clancy lost the wagon and me to him in a poker game or as payment for more whiskey. I don't know which, and I don't care. What I don't like is him approaching you."

"I'll need a plan, and I don't think I'll need the farming equipment in my wagon. I could make room for Bart."

"You certainly will not! We're going to stay at Mike's ranch when we get to Oregon. You hold on to those tools. They're yours, and they can be sold. Don't talk to Bart. He's nothing but trouble. It's not our fault he's only using two oxen and doesn't treat them right. He's never rubbed them down or taken extra time to make sure they had enough water. You hang on tight to what you have, and don't let that man talk you into anything."

Natalie wiped away a tear. "You're the best friend I've ever had, Susan. Thank you for looking out for me."

THE NEXT MORNING, a scream woke Mike out of a dead sleep. He tugged on his pants, jumped out of the wagon, and ran in the direction of the screaming. A small crowd had gathered, and they were all staring at the ground. When he got closer, he could smell the blood before he saw it. The people parted and let him through. There was a big pool of blood just outside the circle of the wagons.

"Everyone back up and let me see what's going on," he instructed. His stomach became a bit queasy. If he was right, this was human blood. Glancing around, he saw drops of blood on the ground. It was still dark out, and he slowly followed the trail. He walked over a small rise and his shoulders sank as he bent his head.

Natalie lay dead on the white ground. A gaping wound across her neck and her empty staring eyes left no doubt she had been murdered. Mike's stomach heaved and he swallowed back bile as he dropped to one knee next to her. The icy chill of death clung to her skin as he closed her eyes and straightened her nightgown so she would be given a bit of dignity in her death. How and what was he going to tell Susan? He didn't need to turn around to know Smitty was behind him. "Don't let anyone else up here just yet."

"Sure thing."

Mike stood and glanced in all directions. The sun was coming up but there didn't seem to be anything to help him to know who had done such a thing. The dry, hard ground revealed no tracks. It wasn't an outsider. It had to have been someone within their camp. If he had to guess, he'd say it was Bart, but he didn't have any evidence, yet.

He hurried back down the rise when he heard Susan's voice calling for him. The anguish on her face physically hurt him. It was a hard blow. He held out his hand and she immediately took it.

"Folks, Natalie Lewis has been killed. She has a broken neck and her throat was cut. It doesn't appear to be the work of Indians."

The crowd had grown increasingly larger, and the collective gasp was loud. He nodded to Eli who had a blanket in his hands and watched him disappear over the slight hill. "I want all men that had guard duty to meet me at Smitty's wagon. Both shifts of guard duty. The rest of you get ready to pull out as usual."

"Aren't we going to lay over a day and find the killer?" Ranger asked.

"No, the livestock need fresh water, and we're a good day's travel until we get there. We'll lay Natalie to rest before we move on."

CHAPTER ELEVEN

*T*he sadness inside her was so vast, Susan couldn't contain it. It seeped over into everything she did, and she felt bad. It had been weeks since Natalie's death, and Susan couldn't find a smile inside of her. She worried about Lily constantly.

They were close enough to the mountains to begin the climb.

On the sides of the trail lay fine pieces of furniture travelers before them must have had to leave behind. Mike warned them they'd need light wagons. She knew one person who was happy: Bart. He was now the proud owner of Natalie's wagon, and the whole situation disgusted her. He gave Mike enough money for the wagon, oxen and everything in it for him to save for Lily when she was found.

Mike didn't want to, but he didn't have much of a choice. As the leader, he was supposed to be impartial, and most seemed to think money set aside for Lily was for the best. Bart hadn't bothered Susan in a week except for an occasional smirk. For the most part, she ignored him.

Mike slowed his horse as he approached their wagon.

"You about ready to stop for the nooning?" He smiled at her and for a moment, her sadness was gone.

"I could use a bit of a rest."

"We'll stop soon." He tipped his hat and rode on down the line of wagons. He'd been so kind and understanding. He held her when she cried, and he treated her with the utmost kindness. It shamed her that she took so much but gave nothing in return. He cared about her, but nothing had changed. He was a wanderer who wasn't ready to settle down.

He'd only grow to resent her, and she didn't want that. No, they'd part as soon as the trip was over. But her future no longer scared her. She was still alive, and she was very capable. She'd get it all figured out. There was no sense borrowing trouble. The wagons came to a stop, and she had things to do. She longed to be away from the whole wagon party but solitude and privacy weren't to be found easily. She started to climb off the wagon when she felt strong warm hands around her waist. Her heart leapt. It was Mike. She knew his touch without having to turn around.

He lifted her down and circled his arms around her middle, drawing her back against him. Somehow, he always knew when she needed his strength.

Closing her eyes, she enjoyed the closeness with him. It was easier to block out the ugliness of the world with him by her side. If only it could last forever. She turned in his arms and laid her ear over his heart. Stolen moments like these were rare. She tried not to be alone with him; he was too much of a temptation. The man she would eventually spend her life with was the man who deserved her virginity. No matter how much she yearned for him, she had to fight her feelings of desire for Mike.

But what if she never met another man she wanted? She

lingered in Mike's arms another few moments and then stepped back. "Thank you for helping me down."

Mike put his finger under her chin and tilted her head until their gazes met. All the desire she felt was reflected back at her in Mike's eyes. Unshed tears pricked her eyes.

She quickly turned and walked outside the circle of wagons. Her need for solitude outweighed her good sense of safety. As soon as she was far enough away that she thought no one could hear she fell to her knees, her body wracked with sobs. Grief bubbled over, and it would not be stemmed. She wept so hard it was nearly impossible to draw a breath.

Mike's hands on her shoulders didn't surprise her. He dropped to his knees, and she fell into his embrace, wrapping her arms around his neck, and he became the port in her emotional storm. The world was so unforgiving with sickness, death, the Indians, and Natalie's killer. Poor Lily was still out there, and she didn't even know her mother was gone. Life wasn't fair, it never had been. Mike rocked her back and forth until she calmed. Cried out, she slumped against his broad chest.

He sat on the ground and pulled her onto his lap. Gently, he brushed her hair out of her eyes. Using the pad of his thumb, he wiped away her remaining tears. His eyes were filled with compassion as he murmured to her. "Honey everything will be fine. I'm here for you."

She stiffened her heart thumped against her chest as she wished she could believe him but life lessons had taught her that his words were untruths. It was nice of him to try though. Eventually she found it easy to breathe again. She began to push away but Mike held her tight.

"Wait, just sit here for a bit, and try to relax. You've been through a lot and I'm worried about you."

"There's no need to worry. Besides you have a whole wagon train full of people you should be worrying about."

KATHLEEN BALL

He kissed the side of her neck, and she shivered. "You're the one I care about. You come first. I've come to care deeply for you, Susan, and there are times when I think you feel the same."

"What do you plan to do once we get to Oregon?" She held her breath waiting for an answer.

"Spend the winter on the ranch and then head back to Independence to lead the next train of people. I can't let my brothers down." He nuzzled her ear making it hard for her to think.

"I understand. I'm hungry, and we should be getting back."

"Let's just stay where we are a bit. I like being alone with you." His husky voice brought an ache to her heart.

She turned in the circle of his arms and gazed up at him. "I know, and that's the problem." Pulling away, she allowed her gaze to linger on his lips for just a moment before she walked alone back to camp. It wasn't his fault. He'd only married her to keep her safe, and he certainly had no other obligation to her. Why couldn't she just be in it for the adventure? Why did she allow her heart to become so entrenched in him?

"Because I'm a damn fool, that's why," she muttered under her breath.

"Susan, come and sit with us for a bit," Savanna called.

"Thanks, Savanna but I have a million things to get done. This evening, I promise."

"I'm going to hold you to that promise." Savanna smiled at her.

Savanna was a woman to admire. Susan hurried to her wagon and fixed bacon and biscuit sandwiches for her and Mike to eat. They'd gotten into a nice routine and he ate most of his meals with her. Smitty often invited them to his fire, and it was a nice treat to spend time with Smitty, Eli, and Jed. Jed missed Lily something fierce. He was the type of man who wore his heart on his sleeve. She often wished she had some words of wisdom for him, but there weren't any.

She ate, occasionally glancing around for Mike, but he didn't come by for his food. She sighed. It was just as well. He knew the outcome same as she did.

As THEY STARTED to travel the upgrade to the mountains, Mike helped many families decide what to leave behind. They still had a ways to go, and they had come to the hardest part of the journey. The oxen were more important than ever. Usually there were a few tears spent when a family heirloom table, chest of drawers, or chair was left behind. The numerous graves they continued to pass made it all too real to the folks.

The only one who refused to give was Big Bart. He had his two wagons now and still all of the oxen he now owned looked to have seen better days. Mike had a sinking suspicion that whiskey wasn't the only thing he had in the wagons. He also had little doubt that Bart was Natalie's murderer, but he lacked the proof necessary to hang him. So he kept a close watch on the man.

Tomorrow they would reach a point where they would have to lower the wagons down a steep mountainside with ropes. He'd find out soon enough how heavy Bart's wagons were. He wasn't about to risk lives for that scoundrel.

Mike worked extra hard each day in the hope he'd tire himself out to the point where he could sleep without tossing and turning, wishing he could lay with his wife. She was the sweetest thing this side of the Missouri, and he couldn't get enough of her. He treasured her smiles the most, since she didn't give them out as readily as before Lily was taken. He doubted they'd ever see Lily again. It weighed on him that Lily's abduction and Natalie's death happened while he was in charge. He didn't take anyone's well-being lightly.

Connie and Ranger had pulled off to the side of the trail and were busy arguing when Mike rode up. They both became awfully quiet all of a sudden.

"Is there a problem?"

Connie flashed her father a look that seemed to be a warning.

"No problem, Mike," Ranger said. "The wagon is a bit heavy and we're trying to peacefully decide what needs to go."

"If you need me let me know," Mike said before he rode off. They were hiding something, too, but he didn't have the time to figure it out. They had to keep going to the next place to camp. It was the only place big enough for them to circle and camp before making their way down the other side of the mountain.

It was hard going for everyone, the drivers and the walkers. There would be more mountains to climb before the trip was through. It was going to be colder in the evenings too. He needed to spread the word for everyone to keep warm tonight. More than once, he watched Jed and Eli dismount and help encourage the oxen to keep going.

Bart's wagons were both stopped in the middle of the trail making it impossible for the others to pass him. The surly man stood wielding a whip, attempting to drive his teams but succeeding only in tormenting the exhausted animals with each crack across their bony backs. That was it; time had come to confront the contrary man. Mike snatched the whip out of Bart's hands and broke it in half. He got down off his horse and led the oxen, pulling the front wagon off to the side. Luckily, the oxen pulling the second wagon followed.

Mike waved the others on by before he confronted the red faced man.

"What in tarnation are you doing? You're whipping the hide right off these poor beasts! You'll not treat animals like this while I'm in charge."

"That's the problem isn't it? You being in charge. I think we need to take a vote and see if we want to continue with you leading us. I bet I could make a good case against you." Bart gave him a smug smile.

"Lighten your wagon before you go any further. I've told you repeatedly to get it done. You're going to kill the livestock, and then you'll be stuck. You and your things will be left behind."

"No one is leaving me behind. No one tells me what to do. You keep putting your nose in where it doesn't belong!"

Mike shook his head. "I'm moving on. I hope you make it to the top but know one thing. If your wagon is too heavy, we're not lowering it down tomorrow. I refuse to risk anyone's life so you can have your whiskey to sell." Mike glanced back at the second driver who shrugged.

"I'll take my whip back," Bart insisted.

"It'll be at the top waiting for you." Mike rode off. There was no use wasting any more time or energy arguing with a man as stubborn as Bart. He'd learn soon enough that there would be no backing down on the rules.

It took all day, but eventually they were up on the top, everyone but Bart. A few members of the party grumbled about it but no one was willing to go back and get him. After most folks had unyoked their livestock, Ranger and his daughter Connie approached him.

"I'm going back to help Bart. Mike, I need you to look after Connie if something happens to me." Ranger shifted his weight from one foot to the other looking decidedly uncomfortable.

"Is there something you want to tell me? Is Bart giving you a hard time?"

Connie started to speak but Ranger told her to hush up.

"No, nothing like that. Just one man helping another. I should be back before dark."

Mike nodded. "I'll look after Connie. You take care of yourself."

Ranger gave him a quick nod and headed off. Mike cocked his brow and gazed at Connie. She didn't say anything. He watched as she made her way back to her wagon. What was really going on?

Mike made the rounds explaining how the wagons would be lowered by ropes. Most looked anxious and it was going to be a very difficult day for all of them. At least no one threatened to turn around and go home. He'd had that happen before, but he'd always managed to get those folks calmed enough to go with the group. It was getting dark and still Big Bart had yet to show. He'd best show soon all men would be needed in the morning to help lower the wagons in the morning.

It was time to spend some time with his wife. He'd miss her when he had to leave again. She might not even stay with him that long. He tried not to think about their parting, but it was inevitable. He halted as he approached their wagon and caught sight of her. Dang, she was a mighty fine woman.

Seated on a crate, bathed in the firelight, she wore a look of serenity he hadn't seen in awhile. It suited her, and he wondered what she was thinking about. It was almost a shame to disrupt her. She turned her head in his direction and smiled. His heart flipped in his chest, and he grinned at her, surprised but pleased when her smile didn't fade.

"I was wondering where you'd gotten to," she said as she poured a cup of coffee for him. She waited until he sat on a crate before handing it to him.

"Thank you." He took a sip. "I was explaining how we're going to lower each wagon down tomorrow."

"Yes, I was discussing it with Clarke and Savanna. Clarke is ready to get it done. I'll have to admit I'm a bit nervous about the whole thing. How will I get down there?"

"People will walk down. There's a footpath not too far away that leads down to the bottom. It zigs then zags so it's not steep. I'm not saying it will be easy but it's not a steep walk. The livestock will have to go down that way too."

"What about the men lowering the wagons? Will they be safe?"

"There's always risk with everything we do on this trip. Having the wagons as light as possible is the key. I'm waiting to see if Bart makes it up the mountain. He was beating the oxen trying to get them to move, and he refused to get rid of anything in those darn wagons of his. Ranger went down to help him." Mike shrugged. "I really don't care if he doesn't join us."

Susan nodded. "He's a horrible man. I know what he did to Natalie. I might not have proof but I know in my gut he did it. But why are both wagon's heavy? Didn't he put some of the whiskey in Natalie's wagon? Just how much whiskey does he have?" She sighed. "Maybe the oxen are too tired out from his lack of care to pull the wagons."

"I agree the oxen are in need of care. And I do agree with you about the whiskey. Either he has a ton of it or there is something else in his wagon. If he makes it up here I'm checking his wagon before we lower it."

"That would probably be for the best. Please be careful. Bart can be mean when he wants to be."

"It's getting late. You'd better head on in and get some rest," he said.

She glanced away, and he couldn't see her expression.

"Good night." She got up and climbed into the back of the wagon.

Had he said something wrong? He didn't seem to know the right thing to say or do lately. Maybe he had never known what to say in the first place. He'd had no business marrying Susan. It was going to be beyond hurtful when they parted.

He sat and watched his brothers remind the men of their guard duty schedule. It was strange but they weren't underfoot anymore. They didn't defer to him before making decisions. They seemed to know what needed to be done, and they did it. Pride filled him as he continued to watch them, but soon that pride was tinged with a bit of sadness that he wasn't as needed as he'd once been. He stood and shook his head. He was acting like an old woman.

He was walking over to Smitty's wagon when Ranger rode up the trail in a cloud of dust as though the very devil was after him. He stopped his horse abruptly at Smitty's wagon and jumped down. "Bart is dead," he announced breathlessly.

He took a few deep breaths. "He had firearms hidden in the wagon—rifles and muskets. He and his driver, Max, had a big fight and Max shot him."

"Where's Max now?" Mike asked.

"They were putting the guns in one wagon and the whiskey in another. They took all of Natalie's things out. I knew when I saw the guns I was in trouble. I didn't say a word, just offered to help. Bart decided to bury the guns. He said you'd just destroy them. Max argued that they could sell them to the Indians, and he thought that was the plan all along. Bart called him stupid. Bart planned to take the guns, the whiskey, and Susan all to California to make money. But because of Mike, he'd just take the whiskey and Susan. He had his eye on the Walton girl and then let it slip in front of me he had plans for my Connie too." Ranger's hands began to shake so he jammed them into his pockets. "I took a step toward Bart, and he pulled his gun. I thought I was dead for sure, but Max shot him clean through the heart. He nodded to me then turned the wagon with the guns in it around and drove off."

Connie came running and threw herself into her father's arms. "Oh, Daddy, you could have been killed."

"I'm fine, sweetheart." He hugged her and then set her away from him. "The oxen are still down there along with the whiskey and wagon. I'm not sure what you want to do."

Mike ran his fingers through his hair.

Eli stepped forward. "I'll take a few of the men and go on down. It's probably best to leave the wagon and take the oxen. We'll bury Bart while we're there. As far as Max goes, let him try to survive with his guns. I doubt he'll get far, and we just don't have the time or manpower to go after him."

Mike nodded, feeling at loose ends. He usually made the decisions. "Sounds like a good plan. Need me to go?"

Eli nodded to something over Mike's shoulder. "I think you're where you need to be."

Mike turned and there stood Susan in her nightgown with a wrap around her shoulders. The moonlight caught the highlights in her dark hair, and she'd never looked lovelier. But she also looked frightened and so very vulnerable. He turned back to Eli. "Sounds like you have everything under control. Let me know if you need me."

Eli nodded. "Will do."

Mike turned once again and strode toward the beauty before him. He gathered her close to him and held on tight, grateful that Bart's plan never came about. A part of him would have died if anything had happened to Susan. The enormity of his feeling for her crashed over him. He wasn't willing to let her go.

"Let's get into the wagon. I need to know you're safe."

Susan nodded. "You'll stay with me won't you?" Her voice wobbled.

"Of course I will." He took her hand and walked with her to their wagon.

SUSAN COULDN'T GET WARM. It was much colder in the mountains. A heat source lay right next to her and she wanted to be in his arms and not only because of the body heat that he provided. Turning onto her side she snuggled against him and smiled when he put his arm around her and pulled her close. Somehow, it always felt wonderful being with him. If she had to pick a man to be with for all of her days, she'd pick Mike.

"The plan Bart had for you scared me. I knew he threatened a few times. I thought...even if he tried, I'd be able to stop him."

"Don't forget Nellie Walton and Connie."

"I don't love Nellie or Connie."

Did that mean he loved her? "Of course you don't." A chilled rolled through her, and she shivered. "It's cold tonight. I'm—"

Mike shifted so she was flat on her back with him looking down on her. He lowered his head until his lips touched hers. She couldn't help but moan, and before she knew it, he'd deepened the kiss. It was beyond any kiss she'd ever experienced. It was almost as though it was full of love. Emotion fluttered in her heart, answering the heat that swept through her body. Still, she hesitated. What if it were all a dream? Or worse, no more than a fleeting moment? He slanted his masculine lips over hers, and all thought left her head as she experienced the feel and taste of him. Coffee and mint; she'd remember that combination the rest of her days. His lips softened as he pressed a bit harder against her. Then she felt it. Desire for this man built in her body so much that it became an ache inside of her. He kissed her neck, and she almost squealed in delight.

She ran her hands over his broad shoulders and his muscled back. He made her feel safe and much cherished. He filled the lonely hole in her heart, and she wished he'd never stop kissing her. But stop he did.

He pulled away and lay on his back, breathing hard. After a moment, he pulled her down so her head lay on his chest, and then he enfolded her in his brawny arms. His heartbeat was loud and fast against her ear. He stroked her back until she drifted off.

When she woke the next morning, her hand automatically went to the empty place beside her. It was too much, trying to keep a distance between them. It wasn't working anyway. Perhaps he'd change his mind and stay with her in Oregon. She dressed and shook her head. No, he wouldn't stay, and she couldn't expect him too. She'd take what time she had with him and be grateful that she'd have memories to live on.

Some of her sadness vanished. It was as though she had found a purpose instead of just drifting from day to day. She was a survivor, and things could be so much worse. No more feeling sorry for herself. Life was for the living, and she needed to stop acting as though she was half dead.

As soon as she placed her last hairpin into her hair, she climbed out of the wagon and smiled. The sun would rise soon, and it was going to be a glorious day. Her smile grew even wider when she saw Mike squatting before the fire smiling back at her.

"It's going to be a good day. I can feel it," she said.

Mike stood and nodded. "It'll be a hard one but good. I

want you to be careful walking down the path. You'll need to lead the oxen." He stepped around the fire and stood in front of her. After the slightest pause, he cupped her face in his hands. "Can you handle that?" He didn't wait for an answer, but instead he lowered his head and placed his lips against hers.

The kiss was almost hesitant at first but it quickly grew into a much deeper kiss until her knees felt weak. Mike was certainly a good kisser. It was almost as though he could communicate his feeling through his kisses. She was being fanciful, but she'd go on being fanciful for as long as she could.

Later, as she walked down the trail, she cringed as she watched the men lower the wagons. She held her breath as each was lowered until they were safely on the ground below. It was a wonder that the first people to travel to Oregon kept going. She would have looked at the drop and thought there was no way to continue with a wagon but there they were, lowering them with ropes.

It took every waking hour to get all the wagons down. The people who got there first made fires and coffee for the rest as they waited for their wagons. It was nice to see everyone getting along for a change. There were no snide remarks or whispers behind hands. They all liked Mike, so they left her alone. The reason shouldn't matter as much, but in a way it did. Trudy even smiled at her, and Susan smiled back. They'd never be friends, but it was nice to not have to cringe every time she saw Trudy.

That night and the next few, Mike came to bed exhausted and barely gave her a peck on the lips before he fell asleep. It was disquieting to lay there with such yearning inside of her.

CHAPTER TWELVE

They were making good time, and Mike was sure they'd beat the snow. The last few weeks had been grueling in so many ways. He decided he had to leave Susan alone. She was a kind, respectable woman, and he had no business kissing her. Part of the reason he'd pushed so hard was he wanted to be dead tired each night. She drew him to her, and it was a great effort to stay away. She'd looked a bit sad and lonely the last week, and he knew he was the cause but it was for the best.

He'd thought of asking her to wait on the ranch while he made trips back and forth as a guide but soon realized it wouldn't be fair to her. She was his sweetness, his heart and his soul. It was so easy to love her. Her beauty shone inside and out.

The creek was cold, but he dunked himself in it anyway. He needed to cool off. The very thing he loved most was pure torture for him. Holding her at night was making him crazy, but he couldn't be without her. He heard a gasp coming from the bank and a smile crept over his face when he saw Susan.

"Howdy. I thought I'd clean off some of the trail dust." He watched as her face grew red. He expected her to run back to the circle, but she stood and stared at his chest.

He took one step then another, revealing more and more of himself as he moved toward her. Still she stared. One more step and she'd see all of him. His stomach fluttered as his heart quickened. He took that step, still standing in the water next to the creek bank. Her staring had such an effect on him, he was forced to cover himself with his hands.

"You can turn around now."

She drew a harsh breath as though she hadn't really known she had been staring. Her hands flew to her face and covered her reddened cheeks. Quickly, she turned around and then ran toward camp.

Mike chuckled. She didn't seem afraid of him. That was good to know. But he longed for her too much. As soon as he got dressed in clean clothes, he volunteered for guard duty. He couldn't lie next to her and not take her. At least not tonight. He'd never find another like Susan, and he didn't even want to try. She was a once in a lifetime love.

IT'D BEEN weeks since Mike had slept next to her, and every morning her heart cracked a bit more. She was afraid it would be completely shattered by the time they reached the Willamette settlements. The loss of Natalie and Lily made it all the more difficult for her to try to be cheerful. Savana lectured her almost every day about keeping her chin up.

Savana had a point. They were lucky to be alive and almost at the end of their journey. Since people were starting to head in different directions to land they had purchased, a dance was planned for that evening.

Sitting up in the early morning, she touched the cold spot

next to her and frowned. No doubt he'd have guard duty while the rest of the travelers celebrated. Savana and Clarke were due to part from the train in two days so this was a good-bye party.

How strange it was that she hadn't known these people before the trip, but now she couldn't imagine being without them. She got out of bed and quickly clothed herself. There was a dress at the bottom of her trunk, and she decided to wear it tonight. It was her very best dress and she bet it was full of wrinkles. After moving around crates and boxes, she finally made it to her trunk. She'd been so frazzled she hadn't thought about wearing the dress for her wedding. She dug deep and frowned when she touched something metal. She pulled up a box, a heavy box, placed it on the floor, and opened it. Her eyes widened. It was full of gold coins. This had to be what Big Bart had been after the whole time. Clancy somehow had stashed gold in their wagon. Maybe it had been Clancy's all along. Rich! She was rich! A bit of laughter bubbled up from inside. She was rich and miserable. Her heart felt as cold as the coins. Carefully, she put the box back where she had found it, took out her green dress, and hung it from the top of the wagon.

Try as she might to keep her mind busy, she couldn't stop wondering about the money. Had Bart known about it? What if he had swapped out the good water for the foul water before Clancy died. That had always bothered her. Bart would have known better than to fill the barrel up with that wretched water, especially since Mike had warned them all. Things began to fall into place. No wonder Bart wanted her dead. She stood in the way of his fortune.

Chills wrapped around her spine. Bart had gotten what he deserved in the end.

Now she had the means to do anything she wanted. She

didn't have to go on to Mike's ranch. It was a lot to think about.

The coffee was ready, bacon was frying, and the biscuits were done. Mike would show up soon. He did it for appearance's sake, and that hurt too. It wasn't his fault. He couldn't help the way he felt, and he'd made it obvious he didn't want or need a wife.

He had a day's growth of whiskers on his face but it only made him all the more handsome. Digging deep, she summoned up a smile and poured him some coffee.

"It was chilly last night," she remarked.

He studied his coffee for a bit before answering. "You'll want to use an extra blanket."

Her heart momentarily stopped. "That's probably a good idea."

"Listen, about the party tonight. Don't wait for me to escort you. I have guard duty. It's the least I can do for everyone."

Everyone but me, she wanted to yell. "Fine." Taking a deep, shuddering breath, she walked away from camp. She needed a bit of privacy and it wouldn't do for anyone to see her tears. It would all be fine. Everything would be fine. Heck, she didn't believe it for a moment. Tears ran down her face, and she didn't try to stem them. There were plenty more to come. In the back of her mind she'd known; she had known it would all end this way, but somehow her heart wouldn't acknowledge it. She was paying the price but the price was much higher than she ever imagined.

Savana called her name, jarring her out of her musings. Quickly she wiped her eyes and walked out to meet her friend. Her eyes were bound to be red and puffy, but there was no help for it.

"I'm glad I found you. Mike was getting worried." Savana reached out and linked her arm with Susan's. "Mike has your wagon all packed and ready to go. I know you're going through a hard time, but no matter what we must keep putting one foot in front of the other. God has a plan for you."

Susan nodded absently and walked the rest of the way herself. Wouldn't it be wonderful if Savana was right? Everything was set and ready, so all she had to do was climb up into the front and drive. A plate with bacon and biscuits was sitting on the bench seat along with her coffee. Mike most probably left it for her. He was nowhere in sight.

They decided to cut the noon stop short so they could stop for the day earlier than usual. Everyone was excited for the dance and eager to get it started. Connie and Trudy both stopped by her wagon, asking if Mike would be attending with her. Their question ate at her until evening.

While everyone else was getting gussied up, Susan decided to do some laundry. She took her green dress down and threw it back into the trunk. There was no sense looking at it. Savana and Clarke were disappointed she'd decided not to go, but they understood. She just couldn't pretend any longer. The first strains of the fiddle twisted around her heart. Someday she'd get over Mike.

First, she'd have to say farewell to the Motts. *One goodbye at a time*. What was her fate to be? She had the means now to do anything she wished. Her shoulders sagged. The gold now belonged to Mike. She shook her head. He wouldn't keep it. Unfortunately, what she wished for didn't have a price tag.

She washed her and Mike's clothes, scrubbing so hard it hurt, but the task distracted her from the celebration. Wiping the sweat off her brow with her sleeve, she sat back on her crate to rest for a moment. It really was a celebration of all their hard work. Some had fared better than others. Some had lost people they loved, and others had found an inner strength they didn't know they had. Life wasn't something one could always control. The number of graves they passed by was testament to that. Things were ever changing.

All she had left to do was empty the water from the tub and then she'd turn in for the night. Taking a deep breath, she held it a moment then let it out slowly. She'd made it through the evening. She stood and dragged the tub away from the wagon. She didn't want a big puddle waiting for her to step in the next morning. It took some doing but she pulled it far enough away. She started to lift one side to allow the water to drain out when she sensed Mike near her. A few more minutes and she'd have been in bed.

He stood behind her then reached around her on each side and took most of the weight of the tub out of her hands. Her heart jumped at his closeness, and she began to shake. It was both heaven and hell having him near.

"You didn't go to the dance."

She ducked under his arm and took a few steps away from him. "No, I thought I'd get ahead on the laundry."

He nodded. "I thought you liked to dance."

"I do but there wasn't anyone I really wanted to dance with. Besides, I don't have reason to celebrate. The people most dear to me were lost or are leaving, and I was never one big on goodbyes. Savana and Clarke deserve to be happy about their new life and not worry about me."

"You have no need to worry. I have the ranch, and you'll be provided for." His brow furrowed.

"Thank you, Mike, for everything. I don't know what I would have done without you. But it's time for me to stand on my own two feet. I have some money set aside, and I'll be fine. We can see a judge first thing and get the annulment before you ride out to your ranch. I could open a boarding house, or well, I don't know but I'm sure I'll be just fine. You have your brothers to look after, and like you said, you're not ready to settle down. I understand." She was proud that her voice didn't waver.

He nodded and his Adam's apple bobbed up and down as though he'd swallowed hard. "Dance with me?" He held out his hand.

She hesitated, but she couldn't deny herself the pleasure of being in his arms. She took his hand and her heart filled with joy when he pulled her into his arms. He was such a good man. A man of great integrity and character, and a man who cared about and for others. He laughed and he encouraged. He loved. Her heart beat faster at the thought of his love but he loved his brothers too and they came first.

They swayed in time to the music her senses filled with everything Mike. He must have taken a dip in the creek. He smelled like soap and leather. Putting her ear to his chest she listened to the thumping of his heart and the feel of his hands stroking her back was lovely. He was by far the most handsome man she'd ever come across and she wanted him to kiss her. She bet he tasted like coffee and mint. Being with him was everything.

The music had stopped but Mike didn't let go. He still swayed with her in his brawny arms for a good while before he dropped his arms and stepped away. It was his way of saying that it was over. She felt it keenly, and she willed herself to smile at him.

"Good night," she whispered before she hurriedly climbed into the wagon. She sat with her back against the side and jammed her fist in her mouth to keep her sobs from pouring out of her. He'd been more than kind to her, and she had no right to make him feel bad.

CHAPTER THIRTEEN

ike squinted against the mid-morning sun as he rode Arrow toward a small group of wagons getting ready to take a different trail. Today the Motts and other were breaking off from the train and Mike went to shake hands and wish them luck. It was always hard to part with friends he made on the trail. With so many life and death moments, they became more like family. He expected to see Susan, but she wasn't there. Puzzled, he scanned the crowd again.

"She already said her goodbyes," Smitty told him. "Looked as though it tore her into pieces. Poor gal. I have to say I had my doubts she'd do well on the trip, but she really was eager to learn and to help. Susan sure is a good woman."

Mike nodded. "Yes, she is. We'll find a judge first thing so I can set her free. She'll be snapped up by someone in no time."

Smitty's left brow cocked. "Are you sure you want to be doing that? I see the way you look at her, and I see the way she looks back at you. Love isn't always convenient, you know, and it certainly doesn't come often. You need to search your heart and soul before you let Susan get away."

"But—"

Smitty shook his head. "Just think about it." He patted Mike's shoulder before he walked away.

It was all he'd been thinking about, and the only thing that made sense was to get the marriage annulled like Susan wanted. It wasn't right to try to hold on to her. Truthfully, if anyone had asked him, he was beginning to want to settle down. He wanted a family and a wife. He wanted to make a go of the ranch but his die had been cast when his parents died. He'd been happy spending his days and nights traveling, but now doubt began to creep in.

He watched the Motts drive off and went in search of his wife. He expected tears but was surprised to instead find her busy packing up the wagon and getting ready to go. She seemed just fine, so he walked in the opposite direction. It had been glorious dancing with her but it was time to let go. In a week, they'd be at their destination and it would be time for them to part.

He glanced to the right when he heard yelling and the next thing he knew he was flat on the ground. Elton Sugarton's horse had just plowed him over. It was painful trying to sit up, and he winced when he moved his arm. A fiery ache shot through his chest and he struggled to breathe against the sharp pressure in his left side. *Dang it!*

Instantly, Eli was at his side. "Let me help you."

"No, don't move me. Get Smitty. I think my ribs are busted and they'll need binding before I move around too much."

Eli nodded and took off in the direction of their wagon. Meanwhile, he felt like a bug being scrutinized, as many of the travelers crowded in around him. Everyone, it seemed, but Susan. Loneliness and disappointment matched his pain until he saw her pushing her way through the crowd.

Just seeing her eased him, and when she knelt next to him and stroked his hair off his forehead with her gentle touch, he wanted to tell her how much he felt for her. He opened his mouth and drew a shallow breath, but before he could utter a single word, Smitty was by his side taking control of the situation. Jed and Eli tried getting everyone to go back to their wagons. Many did as told but a fair amount of onlookers remained.

"Jed, come lift your brother's shoulders for me," Smitty called. "Now just enough so I can get his ribs bound."

Mike closed his eyes against the pain and concentrated on Susan's fingers rubbing his hand. The pain of having his ribs bound was a bad sign. It was definitely a break. Mike moved his arm a bit and was satisfied it wasn't broken, just sprained. He wouldn't be riding a horse anytime soon.

"You're going to have to ride in the back of the wagon," Smitty said as he and Jed got Mike to his feet.

Eli made a path through the crowd, and before Mike knew it he was being set down in Susan's wagon. He groaned out loud. This was the opposite of what he'd intended.

"Are you in pain?" Susan asked. She climbed into the wagon and put every blanket down making as much of a cushion as she could.

"I'll be just fine. A day of rest, and I'll as right as rain."

"We'll take it one day at a time," she responded with a smile.

She sat beside him and buttoned his shirt. Her hands on him were too much. She made him yearn for her in a way he knew he wouldn't be able to fight. "You'll need to drive and do everything yourself."

"Nothing I haven't done before." She leaned over and

kissed his forehead. "I'll try not to hit every bump on the trail. Call out if you need anything."

The smell of lavender lingered well after she climbed out of the wagon.

HE WAS A NICE MAN, but he could make her want to pull her hair out. The last three days had been exhausting, and Mike was nothing but bearish. His impatience with being cooped up was making her crazy. He worried constantly about his brothers, and he didn't seem be able to relax enough to rest.

Now he seemed a bit put out that no one needed him. Both Eli and Jeb were doing a wonderful job leading the rest of the folks. Mike grumbled about the lack questions they had for him. He seemed to be at loose ends, and he took it out on her by being picky about everything. The coffee was either too strong or too weak, too hot or not hot enough. She hit every bump and somehow managed to drive over every rock. The worst was he didn't want any part of her touching him at night. She finally had to put a pile of clothes between them as a barrier.

Now *she* felt grumpy, and there wasn't anyone who she could really talk to. It was a lonely feeling. Lonelier now than it would have been before she'd made such wonderful friends. Lonelier now since the person she loved most in the world had pushed her away. Jed, Eli, and Smitty all helped with the livestock, and they hauled water for her when needed, but they didn't seem to want to be around Mike much. They never visited for too long.

It was the tiptoeing around him that took a toll on her. They were parting in a few days, and that made her want to lash out, but she kept her emotions inside. How long would he take to heal? Did he have someone at the ranch that would take care of him? She sighed. He had his brothers, he didn't need her.

She'd hoped to make a few memories in their last days together but that wasn't going to happen. He'd agreed they should find a judge as soon as they hit town. It would be a big relief to him when she was out of his life. She put the rear of the wagon down so she could make more biscuits for supper. Mike lifted his head and stared.

"Is something wrong? Do you need something?" she asked.

"I need to...well I need to find some bushes to go behind." Crimson seeped into his face.

"I can help you."

His lips formed a grim straight line. "No, get one of my brothers."

She didn't wait to see if there was a please at the end of his order. It would have been futile. So instead, she hunted down Jed and waited with Smitty until Jed returned.

"My brother is one heck of a bear," Jed said, shaking his head. "I don't know how you put up with him."

A lump formed in her throat, but she swallowed hard. "It's only for a few more days. If you'll excuse me, I have things I need to get done." She hurried away, not wanting to hear anything else. She could handle things for a few more days.

But later that night she was done. She couldn't handle her emotions for one more moment. Mike requested more clothes be put between them. Her touch seemed to repulse him, and if she had somewhere else to go she would have. Since she didn't, she just took most of her clothes out of the trunks and piled them up, fortifying the barrier. She turned onto her side facing away from him and gave in to her tears in silence. She couldn't bear it anymore. Not for one more second. She wasn't sure what she had done to make him want her gone, but she had no doubt how he felt.

Two more days. Just two more days, and she could find a place to stay for a while. It was more than his frustration at being disabled. He didn't care for her anymore. It wasn't the first time someone had taken a sudden dislike to her, but never before had it hurt so much. She needed to get out of the wagon and away from Mike. She sat up and as quietly as she could she crawled to the back end.

"Where are you going?"

"Out."

He sighed loudly. "Out where?"

"I just need some fresh air is all. I'll be right outside if you need me." Her voice sounded so wobbly but she couldn't help it.

"That's the problem."

She wished she could see his face but it was too dark. "What's the problem?"

"Never mind. I'm going back to sleep."

Her heart shattered. For a moment, she had thought he was going to say he needed her. Why was she always so hopeful? Why couldn't she be accepting about how people felt? It was her biggest flaw: she was ever hopeful. She scrambled out of the wagon and gulped in the fresh air.

The night was quiet except for the chirping of crickets and the lowing of some of the cattle. The breeze waved through the tree branches, causing shadows to dance in the moonlight. Tilting her head back, she gazed up at the night sky. There were so many stars, and it brought home the fact that whatever she was going through was minor compared to the suffering of others. Her grief would pass someday. The best thing she could do for everyone was to act as though she was excited for the next chapter of her story. She'd be bound to see some of the people from the train in town from time to time and she didn't want pity or whispers.

She could pull it off for the sake of Eli and Jed. They

needed the security Mike gave them. They relied on him, and she didn't want to be the cause of any rift between them. Smitty, on the other hand, wouldn't be fooled, but she was pretty sure he wouldn't tell anyone about her sadness. Smitty always wanted what was best for the brothers.

There were plenty of men in the world, and she'd just have to find one who loved her and wanted to make a life with her. Now that she had money, she could afford to be choosy. No more instant weddings for her. She took a deep breath and let it out slowly, calming herself. As soon as her tears dried, she crawled back into the wagon and drifted to sleep.

CHAPTER FOURTEEN

*M*ike knew the town was in sight by the excited conversations going on all around. People called from wagon to wagon congratulating one another. He smiled. Another safe journey accomplished, even if it did end with him flat on his back. He and his brothers were all in one piece. Now all he wanted to do was go out to his ranch and recuperate there.

His smile faded as his heart squeezed. It was going to be hard to get over Susan. There would never be any woman like her. He'd never love so deeply again. He could feel it and he wished he could just shrug it all away and ride it out. The road without her threatened to be beyond bumpy.

The wagon slowed then stopped. He heard Susan pull the break and scramble down from the seat. People hurried past, probably anxious to see the town. He often wondered where the people of his party would end up. He'd been surprised over the years. Some he thought above reproach ended up working at the saloon. Others decided that the gold in California was a better bet. A few times people discovered they had bought land that was already owned. Unfortunately, there always seemed someone ready to take advantage of others no matter what the situation was.

There always seemed to be one or two couples who had fought the whole way there then ended up united in marital bliss. Dang it! His line of thinking was making things worse. One more night, and he'd be able to ride away. He wished he could ride away and not look back but he had a feeling he'd be looking back for the rest of his life.

The wagon jostled slightly as Susan climbed into the back.

"Why aren't you heading to town?" he asked. "It sounds like everyone else is."

"They are. I wanted to see how you fared. It was a bumpy ride the last few miles. Can I get you anything? I'll get a fire going and put the coffee on." She turned to leave but he grasped her hand.

"Don't go just yet. I have so much to thank you for." The smile that had just lit up her face faded until sadness filled her eyes.

"It's me who needs to be thanking you. I appreciate everything you did for me. If you think you can wait a little bit, I bet I can find the judge. Your obligation to me will be over, and we can both go on with our own lives." She withdrew her hand from his and left.

Darn it! If he was lucky, the judge would be gone for a long while. He rubbed his hand over his face and shook his head. It would give him nothing but more pain to think that way. He had promised to let her go, and he'd honor his promise.

Susan stared at the aging sheriff. He had a full beard, white as snow, and his face looked like old leather. "What do you mean the judge is gone? When will he be back?"

The sheriff stood behind his desk. "When I said gone, I meant dead. I meant we have no judge, and we most likely won't see one unless we have a major problem."

"What would a major problem be?" She just wanted to get everything over with.

He shrugged and tugged on his beard. "A hangin' offense. Other than that, we don't need one. Is there something I can do for you?"

"I don't suppose you can annul a marriage?"

His eyes widened. "An annulment? Look Miss—uh, I mean Missus. Most people in this community won't take kindly to a divorced woman."

"It's not a divorce. It's an annulment." Heat washed over her face.

"Same thing too many in this town. Do yourself a favor and stay married to your man. That is unless he beats you." He leaned forward, peering at her through squinted eyes. "Does he beat you?"

"No, nothing like that."

"Was he already married?"

Annoyed, Susan shook her head and snapped, "No."

"Well, then, there you go. You probably shouldn't get unhitched anyway. If you want, you can wait for a judge to pass through, but take my advice, you'll be rejected by many women in town. They are mostly a good lot, but they are a bit particular about a person's character." He came out from behind his desk and walked to the door. He opened it and nodded at her. "You have a good day, ma'am.

She walked out the jailhouse and down the long wooden boardwalk, feeling as though she was walking in fog. Nothing was clear to her. She couldn't bear to be judged by people again. She couldn't stay married either. It just wasn't the deal she struck with Mike. There had to be a way to be unmarried without others knowing they'd been married.

She passed Nellie Walton on the walkway and nodded. No, too many people knew of her situation. Too many people loved to gossip. It all seemed so simple when she had asked Clancy to marry her. How was she going to tell Mike? He was sure to be hopping mad. She strolled to the end of the walk and stared at their wagons, all nicely circled. They'd come a long way. Most had made it but she still felt heartsick about Natalie and worried about Lily. Mike told her that if Lily didn't cause trouble for her captors, she would live as either a slave or a wife, and that life wouldn't be easy. And that she would most likely die a very young woman if she made it that long. The poor girl.

How big was Mike's ranch? Maybe there was a spot where she could build her own house. A spot where she was far enough away that she wouldn't see him every day. She'd had months and months to figure out a plan, and here she did not know the first thing to do. She bit her bottom lip dreading going back and telling Mike. Maybe she could just tell him she saw the judge and everything was done. She shook her head as she stepped off the walk onto the hard packed dirt. No, that wouldn't work. She'd just have to tell him the truth and hope he didn't want to kill her. She'd earn her keep or maybe next spring she could go somewhere else to live.

No, that was the answer. Why wait? She'd leave as soon as possible.

Spotting Mike sitting on a crate next to their fire surprised her. She stopped short a few feet away and stared at him, drinking in the sight of him. "Hey."

"Hey, yourself." He smiled.

"Should you be sitting? Are you in pain?" She wished she could go and touch him; just to be sure he was fine.

"It's a little painful but the fresh air is exactly what I needed. Don't worry, Smitty helped me."

"Shall I help you back?"

He laughed and then winced. "Ow, are you trying to get rid of me?"

"Of course not. In fact, we have to talk, and you're not going to like what I have to say. I went into town and there is no judge. He died, and the sheriff said we won't see one for a while. I can't un-marry you right now, but I do have a plan." He started to say something and she put her hand up to stop him. "Just listen to me. This is for the best. I'm going to buy supplies and head to the next town or the town after that. I don't know yet but I'll go somewhere you won't be, and I'll send word where I end up. People won't care if you have the marriage annulled, but they will care if I do. As soon as the judge comes to town have him draw up the papers or whatever needs to be done and send them to me. This is for the best. You don't want to settle down, and I don't want an absent husband. I thank you from the bottom of my heart for all you've done for me. I'm not going to allow you to be saddled with me for the rest of your life." She swallowed hard, not able to go on.

His face became expressionless, and when he spoke, his voice was carefully even. She couldn't read him. "Is that what you want?"

"I think it's what we both want. My impulsiveness led to our predicament, and I'm so sorry. It all seemed so easy at the time. It never occurred to me what other people would think about us ending the marriage. I certainly won't be a woman of good standing if people knew. I plan to leave in the morning."

He nodded and looked away. Why wouldn't he look at her? Maybe he was just relieved and didn't want her to know.

"I have some money I'd like to give you as your pay. You played your part well."

Mike struggled to stand and then he stared right at her. "I played my part well, and you want to pay me?" He sounded incredulous. He turned and slowly walked away as her heart dropped to her feet.

What had she done wrong? She watched him walk slowly toward town. He was probably going to see about getting a judge to come sooner. What she needed was information. Where was the next town, and would it be safe for her to travel alone? Maybe she could hire someone to take her, but who?

Ideas always sounded so simple, but putting a plan into action wasn't easy. In fact, it was near infuriating.

"Where's Mike?" Smitty's voice startled her. She hadn't heard him come up behind her.

She sighed. "He walked to town. Oh, Smitty, I've made a terrible mess of everything."

Smitty gestured toward the fire. "Let's have a sit down and talk this out."

She nodded and quickly sat on one of the crates. "There isn't a judge."

Smitty's brow furrowed. "What happened to Judge Green?"

"The sheriff said he was dead. I'm sorry, was he a friend of yours?"

Smitty nodded. "We've known each other since we were kids." He looked away for a moment and then turned back toward her. "So what is the problem?"

"I promised Mike an annulment when we got to town. Now that isn't going to happen. I offered to pay him for pretending to be my husband, and he left. I don't understand."

Smitty smiled. "You know, Mike never does anything he

doesn't want to."

"Mike doesn't plan to settle down, and I don't plan to live my life away from my husband." She balled her hands into tight fists. This was getting her nowhere.

"All I know is you two have been making calf eyes at each other for a long while. If Mike hadn't planned to stay married, he'd have never slept in your wagon. And don't tell me he did it to quiet the loud group of nosey hens we had traveling with us. We have a group like that each trip." He stood up. "Open your heart to him, and see what happens. You have nothing to lose at this point."

Smitty's advice only led to her feeling queasy. Nothing to lose? She watched him head back to his wagon. She'd already lost. The sooner she left the better. She'd be making another trip immediately.

MIKE STRODE across the boardwalk and pushed open the saloon doors, holding his aching ribs. He scanned the room, seeking his wife. The saloon was a long shot, and he figured Sven at the stable was mistaken about seeing a woman of her description heading for the local watering hole. The brittle tones of the piano playing a lively tune mingled with raucous laughter. Women in garish feathers and bright silk lounged with some of the men in the crowded place.

He spun on his heel, ready to walk back the way he'd come. His wife was definitely not—

And there she was, at the end of the bar, looking uncomfortable, addressing a shifty character sitting on a barstool. At least she didn't look comfortable. Her face was red, and she clasped her hands in front of her.

"I can pay!" she insisted.

"Slim, isn't going anywhere with you," Mike said as he

joined them. Gingerly, conscious of his painful ribs, he slid his arm around Susan's waist. "She's my wife."

Slim's eyes grew wide. "Shame on you, trying to run out on your husband!"

Wearing an expression of mortification, Susan pried Mike's arm off her and hurried out of the saloon.

Mike shook his head as he hurried after her. Dang it, chasing after her wasn't doing his ribs any good, but he walked quickly to catch up to her. "Susan, we need to talk."

She stopped in front of an alley and jammed her hands on her hips. Before she could get a word out, Mike took her by one hand and pulled her into the alley. He walked them into the shadows and turned her so her back was against the side of a building. She was a sight when she was all spitfire mad.

He swooped down and captured her lips with his. She was still talking as he deepened the kiss. All at once, the fight went out of her and she was kissing him back. Her lips were delectable and he was amazed at how silky her skin was as he cupped her face in his hands.

They came up for air, but Mike kissed her again. He'd never get enough of her. Deep down he'd known it from the start. She was a part of him. Susan held claim to a big portion of his heart, and he wasn't going to lose her.

"I think we're good together," he said as he ended the kiss. He caressed her cheeks with his hands. "I don't want you to go. If you go, you'll be tearing me in two. I know it wasn't what you planned for your life, but I'm asking you to stay with me."

Her eyes misted as she stared at him. "For how long? Until the winter is over? Then what I'm supposed to live without you for the rest of the year? I'd be worried the whole time you were on the trail. Maybe I'm being selfish. I just don't know."

He leaned down and kissed her again. "I'm asking you to

be my wife. I've had nothing but time to think these last days. Eli and Jed are ready to go on without me. I'll worry of course but Smitty will be with them. Sometimes I can see Eli chaffing to take charge. Besides, I have all winter to make sure they know everything. I need you with me. I love you with everything inside of me. It's time for me to make a go of the ranch and have it profitable enough for Eli and Jed to settle down too, one day." He took her hands in his. "Please say yes."

Her eyes grew wide, and she stared at him. Then she stood up on tiptoe, wrapped her arms around his neck, and pulled him down for a kiss. It was the sweetest kiss he'd ever had. It was full of love, and commitment, and yes.

She stepped back. "Oh no, I forgot about your ribs. I need to get you back to camp."

"Well?"

"Well what?"

"Will you marry me?" He swallowed hard and waited.

"I love you more than words can say. So yes, of course." Her smile cast away the shadows.

EPILOGUE

"I can't believe all this land is yours," Susan said. She sat on the wagon bench with Mike as he drove the oxen. "A person could get lost out here."

"That they could. You'll see as we get closer. There's the bunkhouse and the barn. It's almost like civilization."

She smiled and put her hands around his powerful bicep. "I can't wait. It seems like we were at that boarding house for a month instead of a week. I know the doctor wanted you to rest longer, but I'm glad to be on our way."

"I can't wait. Look there." He pointed. "See, nestled under the trees? It's hard to see from here but that's the house."

Excitement filled her. "I can't wait to see it. Does it have curtains? Maybe we should have bought a few things before coming out."

"We're not so far from town. You can go to the mercantile and put whatever you like on my account."

"I have my own money."

He slowed the wagon and looked at her, taking on a serious tone. "We don't know who that money belongs to, and until we do I think it best not to spend it."

"You always have to be so logical about things," she teased.

"I'm not logical where you're involved. My heart beats faster whenever you're near and all thought leaves me it seems."

"You're quite a charmer." She stopped talking when they drew up near the house. It was much bigger than she'd expected. It was two stories and it seemed to sprawl on and on. "Oh my."

"We built it all ourselves," Mike said, and the pride in his voice was unmistakable.

He parked the wagon in front of the house, jumped down and was immediately at her side waiting to help her down. She put her small hand in his big one and squealed when he swung her up into his arms.

"You'll hurt your ribs," she protested.

"We're going to do at least one thing traditionally. I'm carrying you over the threshold."

She glanced around and saw Eli, Jed, and Smitty watching from the barn. They all had knowing smiles on their faces, and she grew warm inside.

Mike fumbled with the door for a moment before he got it opened. Then he carried her inside and set her on her feet. Immediately she headed toward the back of the house.

"Where are you going?" he asked as he clasped her hand.

"I want to look around."

He pulled her into his strong arms and kissed her so tenderly she wanted to cry. Her heart filled with joy, more than she would ever have thought possible. She was lucky to have such a fine man as Mike.

"I'll show you the house later. First, I want to show you our room." He gave her a wicked smile, and her face heated.

"It's daytime, and we already did that." She stared at the floor.

"I thought you enjoyed it."

"Well, I did, but I'm a decent woman."

"Susan look at me. You are a decent woman. You're a good, kind, smart woman, who I want to love. Right now. In our house."

The love in his eyes was unmistakable, and her protests melted away. "All right but just this once."

Mike threw back his head and laughed. "Oh my dear, we've only just begun."

THE END

I'm so pleased you chose to read We've Only Just Begun, and it's my sincere hope that you enjoyed the story. I would appreciate if you'd consider posting a review. This can help an author tremendously in obtaining a readership. My many thanks. ~
Kathleen

ABOUT THE AUTHOR

Sexy Cowboys and the Women Who Love Them...
Finalist in the 2012 and 2015 RONE Awards.
Top Pick, Five Star Series from the Romance Review.
Kathleen Ball writes contemporary and historical western
romance with great emotion and
memorable characters. Her books are award winners and
have appeared on best sellers lists including: Amazon's Best
Seller's List, All Romance Ebooks, Bookstrand, Desert
Breeze Publishing and Secret Cravings Publishing Best
Sellers list. She is the recipient of eight Editor's Choice
Awards, and The Readers' Choice Award for Ryelee's
Cowboy.
Winner of the Lear diamond award Best Historical Novel-
Cinders' Bride
There's something about a cowboy

 facebook.com/kathleenballwesternromance

twitter.com/kballauthor

instagram.com/author_kathleenball

OTHER BOOKS BY KATHLEEN

Lasso Spring Series

Callie's Heart

Lone Star Joy

Stetson's Storm

Dawson Ranch Series

Texas Haven

Ryelee's Cowboy

Cowboy Season Series

Summer's Desire

Autumn's Hope

Winter's Embrace

Spring's Delight

Mail Order Brides of Texas

Cinder's Bride

Keegan's Bride

Shane's Bride

Tramp's Bride

Poor Boy's Christmas

Oregon Trail Dreamin'

We've Only Just Begun

A Lifetime to Share

A Love Worth Searching For

So Many Roads to Choose

The Settlers

Greg

Juan

Scarlett

Mail Order Brides of Spring Water

Tattered Hearts

Shattered Trust

Glory's Groom

Battered Soul

The Greatest Gift

Love So Deep

Luke's Fate

Whispered Love

Love Before Midnight

I'm Forever Yours

Finn's Fortune

Glory's Groom